T0278484

THE SLOVAK LIST

Series Editor: JULIA SHERWOOD

The Slovak List introduces works by writers from Slovakia, a country whose literature has so far remained in the shadow of its neighbours in Central Europe and not available to a wider readership. Launching with books by contemporary women authors, the series will feature work that reflects the diversity, innovation and variety of themes covered by Slovak writing today as well as in the recent past.

The Slovak List is supported by SLOLIA, the Centre for Information on Literature in Bratislava, Slovakia.

SEAGULL BOOKS
•
CELEBRATING 40 YEARS

ZUSKA KEPPLOVÁ

The Moon in Foil

TRANSLATED BY MAGDALENA MULLEK

LONDON NEW YORK CALCUTTA

Slovenské
literárne
centrum

This book was published with the financial support
of the SLOLIA Board, The Slovak Literary Centre.

u.
slovak
arts
council

Supported using public funding by the Slovak Arts Council.

Seagull Books, 2023

Originally published in Slovak as *Buchty švabachom*
© Zuzana Kepplova / LITA, 2011

First published in English translation by Seagull Books, 2023
English translation © Magdalena Mullek, 2023

ISBN 978 1 80309 254 6

British Library Cataloguing-in-Publication Data
A catalogue record for this book is available from the British Library

Typeset by Seagull Books, Calcutta, India
Printed and bound in the USA by Integrated Books International

CONTENTS

You Can Be Not Afraid

PETRA, PARIS

ANKA, LONDON

MIKA, HELSINKI

Trianon–Delta

You Can Be Not Afraid

PETRA, PARIS

Paris, Bratislava . . . Water, Water Everywhere

'Central Pool's been torn down,' Petra's father said before the Skype connection broke again. For a while Petra kept repeating 'Can you hear me?' into the microphone, then she took off her headset and closed her laptop. She went to the window and checked whether her swimsuit was dry yet. Synthetics dry in no time. Then she opened her laptop again and typed the keywords 'bratislava pools' into Google.

Those two words had been key for her for quite some time. She had spent her childhood at the Central Pool. When she would close her eyes at night, she could still see the neon lights and the plastic bars of the pool building's ceiling. She spent early mornings and entire afternoons in chlorinated water. The last time she was in Bratislava, she had gone to the Central Pool. She snuck onto the grounds through a gap in a corrugated metal fence. The stucco was peeling, and for the first time Petra realized that the building was made of brick. She had always thought it was made of plastic. A strong wind would have been enough to lift it and set it down in a tower

block area of any postsocialist town. It was an easily sub-
stitutable block dropped in between the marketplace and the
Istropolis building, smelling like a coffee roaster and the Stein
brewery on one side, and like the Figaro candy company on
the other. It occurred to her that the Central Pool being torn
down made her an old-timer. From now on she could annoy
young people with detailed descriptions of things that have
been and would never be again.

Skype rang, a green and a red handset appeared on the
screen. A gust of wind shut a roof window, and it started to
rain again. The swimsuit slipped off the line into a bucket and
splashed into water. Petra saw it happen, but she quickly
reached for the headset and pressed the green button: 'Dad,
are you there?' There was silence. Water leaking through the
ceiling started to drip into buckets spread around the room.
It dripped in different keys, depending on the water level in
each bucket. Petra sat down on the bed and listened to the
sound.

A National Wafer

Once a month she went to the post office to pick up a package. The box was always filled to the brim with Horalky wafers. 'Horalka is the only honest sweet!' her mother would say. 'No so-called improved recipe, no 20 per cent more free, or any other capitalist lies!' For the last 20 years Petra's mother brought home the same sweets every time she went grocery shopping. As a result, she critiqued societal change with the vocabulary of wrappers, brands, and weights. She'd set her bags down on the table, unload the groceries, turn on Regina radio, and as she fried onions until they were translucent, she'd criticize the state of society. Since everyone was coming together for dinner, or just passing through the kitchen, Petra's mother had an audience. 'We're a kitchen nation!' she'd call after the passers-by who were grabbing scissors, looking into the bags, or sampling the food in the pots. 'Slovaks have never sat in drawing rooms, they've always sat on a stool in the kitchen!' It made Petra laugh every time. 'Mom, you're our Slovak Heritage Institute,' Petra's father would say to her and smack her bum. Her brother Michal would usually add that they had a Hungarian last name, so they probably did sit in that drawing room.

Petra's mother wasn't much for sophisticated arguments, but when she unpacked the old-time wafers, she could back up her political views. 'Look!' She held the package between her fingers to show the true size of the product. 'This is how they cheat us!' And there was no arguing with that. No one dissented, everyone sat down around the table, and she served the meal. Meanwhile she ranted about the invisible hand of the market, which was stealing food from her pots. 'They'll cook us like that frog from the story! Slowly, gradually, we won't even notice. As if we were stupid! And every night they brazenly tell us that we're better off, we just don't want to admit it!' Michal kicked Petra under the table. He was worried that their mother would start riding the trams, plastic bag in hand, waving her fist, and speaking to some obscure group of conspirators. Like the woman who got undressed in the park, and then an ambulance took her away. 'If they ever make Horalky smaller or change some ingredient, Mom will lose it,' he said to Petra, laughing.

Every month she opened the box and looked over the wafers. She always ate Horalky after swimming. She'd hold the hairdryer in one hand, and the wafer in the other. The body reacted to the sugar, so she was always in the best mood after swimming. The world made perfect sense, it smelt clean like chlorine, it swayed in the rhythm of splashing flip-flops, it tasted like a wafer that hadn't changed for years. When Michal left for Finland, two packages went out every month— one to Paris, the other to Helsinki. He emailed Petra: 'Yesterday was the first time my Turkish colleague got a bite of Horalky. He said it tasted like one of their traditional Turkish wafers, but that theirs was better.' 'Did you know that *bryndza* in Romanian means cheese? It's just their word for cheese,' Petra wrote back. They agreed they wouldn't tell their mother. Then they exchanged a lot of smiley faces.

Like Caryatids

'I want to tell you something. I'll tell you because you're leaving. I'm not from Greece, I'm Albanian.' Petra was leaving the hotel, and a stout Greek woman was taking her place. Her figure reminded Petra of caryatids, female statues that supported the roof of a temple on their heads. The woman wasn't just well built and evenly covered in a layer of soft fat, she was also quite muscular. An ideal worker.

Petra showed her what each cleaning product was for. She recommended that the Greek woman wear gloves, even though her hands would still smell of them in the morning as she broke her baguette, Here, Petra let her smell her fingers. She also reminded the Greek woman that she could take home the leftovers from the hotel—old bread, little packets of butter, jam, and honey—but she'd have to work it out with the other women. Petra was just lifting a mattress to show her a trick to making the bed.

'Do you do sports?' the Greek woman asked when she saw Petra's biceps. 'I swim. I'm going to work as a swim instructor. Alongside my studies.' After working at the hotel all summer, Petra had enough money for tuition, and the swimming lessons would give her pocket money during the school year. Her parents always sent her something as well. 'I'm a junior judo champion,' the Greek woman said. 'That's good, you'll stay in shape here,' Petra said, laughing. 'Take a look at the African mamas that work here, every one of them is built like an armoire!' The Greek woman misinterpreted Petra's words of encouragement. 'Those of us who have been training since we've been little know what hard work is, don't we?' Then she asked about money; she had a lot of questions about money. As if those questions were a way of going through Petra's pockets, squeezing her cheeks, and checking the fat on her fingers, to make sure that she was well fed and in good shape after the three-month stint.

An elevator full of laundry bags took them down to the hotel basement. They walked down the hallways to the laundry. Petra added a key to the room with the washers and dryers to the Greek woman's key ring. 'It's good you're going to study,' the Greek woman said. 'Otherwise you'll never be one of them. If we stopped serving them, they'd have no one to cook for them, do their laundry, or take care of their children, wouldn't you say?' With that mysterious *they*, the Greek woman reminded Petra of her mother. 'I won't teach them to swim then!' she said, laughing. The Greek woman liked Petra. She ran on endorphins. A substance that fuels people who are always on the move. Not letting it get you down, that was the secret to this work. Grumpy employees got fired. Always with a smile. A genuine one. 'They think all we do is cheat and steal!' the Greek woman said.

The previous summer a friend came to see Petra and spent a few nights with her. When the friend left, Petra found a 20-pound banknote under her laptop. Her childhood friend had worked in England. She had a degree in social work, but she went to pick strawberries in England. She'd get on her folding bike, ride to the station, put a lock on her bike, and cover the seat with a Tesco bag to protect it from sunlight and dew. Then she'd get on a bus that would take her to a low-cost flight. When she got back, she would unlock the bike and pedal home. That summer she stopped by Petra's, looked around Paris, and took a break from rainy London. Petra prepared her a bed & breakfast, as Anka called it. One time they got drunk together, and Anka said that if all the immigrants and seasonal workers stopped doing what they did and actually went where the locals so frequently sent them, their entire clean society would drown in trash. 'A more apocalyptic film hasn't been made yet! We're not talking about the head of the Statue of Liberty on the pavement! We're talking about a morning when all the coloured and non-coloured people from Eastern Europe pack their bags and go bye-bye!' The friend had such a mistrust of banks that she always carried around several months of her earnings in cash in her backpack. Banknotes with the head of the queen stuffed into a plastic bag, and the plastic bag in a cloth backpack. The reality was that the banks didn't trust her, and no one would have opened an account for her. With her cash she travelled across Europe, from north to south; she was her own auto-payment system.

Petra didn't want to think like that. She didn't want to be angry as she was loading a washing machine, as she pushed a basket of linens, as she put on her rubber gloves. In the morning she found the 20-pound banknote under her laptop. You don't pay to stay with friends, she thought. And her friend had broken that rule. She pulled a queen out of her backpack and stuck it under the computer. Petra thought that Anka had gone mad on the isles. And then there was the Greek woman, smiling and strong, but distrustful and using the magical *they*. With strong hands and red cheeks, like a worker from a socialist monument. Petra carried bags, swam, and in September she was going to start school. She had a plan, which made her feel like she didn't want to participate in grumbling or blaming. She was going to wear a white coat and officially be useful to society. 'A doctor will never be lost, everyone will always need doctors,' Petra's father used to say. 'They just don't always get paid for it,' Petra's mother would add.

'Petrushka, I marvel at you young people, how you go out to work like that, of your own free will,' Petra's grandma had said to her before she left for Paris. 'Intelligent young people! I understand that you want to have your own money and be independent, but at the cost of wiping butts in Austria? Old grandpa, when he had to work with his hands, he stopped talking. In the '50s, they put a doctor of philosophy to work at a factory! Every night he came home, lay down on the couch, and stared at the ceiling. Without saying a word. I had to force him to eat dinner. We walked around on eggshells at home, but I was glad that he didn't beat me or your mother, because elsewhere the family took the brunt of it. He was the type of person who kept it all inside. They made him carry heavy loads, and when one of them got crushed, those dumb proletarians summoned your grandfather, since they thought he was a doctor. They didn't even know how to add or divide the money for wages, because they had sent the accountants to work as boiler operators!'

The Greek woman asked Petra whether she could call her if she ran into a problem or got sick. 'I don't know anyone here yet.' Petra said yes, though she had no idea how she'd get her medication without a prescription. 'Why don't you get a temporary worker number for health insurance? They'll ask you for it here at work. You can't get a job without it!' They had hired the Greek woman in a hurry as a replacement for Petra. She promised to bring the required papers soon. 'I'll tell you because you're leaving. I'm not from Greece, I'm Albanian,' the Greek woman said. She had no papers. She was going to try to stretch it as long as possible. And either they'd keep her on as an illegal worker, or she'd get herself Greek papers.

If she ended up working illegally, she'd carry cash home in her backpack like Anka. She'd be on her guard on the bus, at the airport, on the plane, so she wouldn't fall asleep and her backpack wouldn't disappear. London–Bratislava, Paris–Tirana. With no sleep. Petra wondered what the Customs agents would say when a backpack full of money went through the X-ray machine. Would they question her in a small room and fill out a long form? Would dogs sniff her? Would she be subjected to a cavity search? She had forgotten to ask Anka where she kept her money the whole time. At home in a suitcase? Or in a safe at the train station? She handed the Albanian woman another key, to a locker for clothes and personal items. The metal box looked as if it came from a changing room where athletes change before practice. She warned the new employee not to keep valuables there. Then she wished her good luck and squeezed her hand tight. The Albanian woman clung to her shoulder and hugged her.

It was a hug for good luck with a pat on the back, just like when two players are trading out.

Petra felt as though she and the Albanian woman were close after having walked all over the hotel together. At the same time she hoped the Albanian wouldn't call her. She didn't understand why she felt that way. It was just a feeling. A feeling that she was done with the hotel. She was going to school and soon she'd be teaching kids to swim. When she looked back at the hotel and waved at her former colleagues who were smoking by the service entrance, she thought about caryatids again, strong women standing around the entrance. *Hello kids, I'm from Greece* . . . a jingle popped into her head, and the only thing that got rid of it was the din of the metro.

Wild Nights

A towel over her face, a few more breaths through the terry cloth, and then a stream of water that didn't let her breathe any more. She attempted to inhale a few times, but the water kept pouring onto the towel, which was getting heavier, and she couldn't take another breath. She could feel her toes stretch and flail, then her whole leg jerked. She was losing control over her muscles. The towel made it impossible to take another breath. It enveloped her face like a mask made of hardening white terry cloth. For a brief moment she forgot that she was in the showers at the pool. Her swimming colleagues were standing over her. They were pouring buckets of water onto her face covered by a towel.

It brought back a memory, just a tiny fragment, not a whole one, of a similar feeling when she used to sleep in an apartment with beds pushed up against one another. One time, there was an American couple that had stopped in Paris during their trip across Europe. To them, Europe meant London, Paris, Rome, and Madrid. For a while they slept in a park, then she invited them to their apartment. They needed to get a roommate for a few weeks to help pay the rent. Then there was a Czech girl who had spent her days in Paris, the city of fashion, sitting on her bed, flipping through glossy magazines. A month later she gladly went home and left a vacant bed. And then there were all of Natália's men. Petra's bed was right next to hers. A few times she woke up because she was breathing into the face of some man who was lying between her and Natália. Other times she woke up because of a dream in which she couldn't breathe; she would talk in her sleep, then she'd start and sit up. She'd immediately forget her dream, but her heart would be racing. At home she had had no trouble sleeping. She'd still have one foot on the ground, and she was already asleep. Her dreams were mostly ordinary, shreds of reality, assembled in comical ways. And all of a sudden she was waking up to her own voice. It was as if loud breathing were transforming into words, and back again. She felt a little embarrassed. Nightmares in the middle of an apartment full of sleeping people. She opened her eyes and saw curtains over a French window, and a small window above the beds that was cracked open. There must have been too little air for the number of people in the apartment.

She tore the towel off her face and saw the swimmers' faces over her. She was lying on the tile floor in the shower. Someone had come up with the idea to try waterboarding. Simulated drowning. Something new from prisons populated by alleged terrorists. Petra and her swimming colleagues spent a few hours a day in the water. They couldn't believe that a wet towel over the face could really frighten someone. They were looking into Petra's eyes: her pupils narrowed as soon as she took off the towel. She sat up quickly and wiped the water off her face. The flashback of the apartment she had lived in after arriving in Paris was gone. Someone took Petra's spot on the tile floor. They handed her a bucket of water. Now she'd get to be the one doing the drowning.

The brief moment under the towel had given her a sense of what her bad dreams would be about for the rest of her life. To this day her mother still occasionally travelled to Russia in her dreams. She would be packing and unpacking suitcases, running late for her train, rushing to the bathroom with no walls between the stalls, and in line in front of her stall Russian women would be banging on her door, she would look down and see two footprints on a white board, all of a sudden there'd be no seat, just a hole in the ground covered with flies, and someone would hand her a newspaper to wipe herself, and then she'd be running for the train again . . . Her mother always laughed when she retold that dream. She'd always add a few stories from dorms or spas, a couple of jokes. But at the same time she'd say that after every such dream she woke up in a sweat and had to change her nightgown.

Now Petra knew the subject matter of her future dreams. She'd have her own dorm room, a regular income from swimming lessons, she'd get a French boyfriend, and fall asleep next to him. But a couple of times a year she'd wake up and go change her sweaty nightgown. She'd try to recall the dream, and at breakfast, with a croissant and a stick of butter, she'd tell her boyfriend how she used to sleep in a room full of people. The air was stale, it was the middle of the summer, in the centre of Paris. There were crumbs on the table, and the butter was melting. Not far away there was a train station, ambulances and fire trucks kept flying by. In a window across the street firemen were doing pull-ups. Once in a while someone shouted on the street. The hot asphalt brought over the smell of the Pakistani neighbourhood, where the stores had vegetables in shapes you couldn't dream up, where the food in the kiosks was so spicy that you couldn't get down a single bite of it, and the Pakistani men never shouted at the women, they just stood on the pavement and talked, they had soft voices, which mixed with the sounds of the city, thickened into a porridge, got thicker and thicker, until the mixture became too heavy, it needed to be stirred around in the dreams so that it wouldn't stick to your brain. A leg would jerk involuntarily, the body would stretch, and Petra would go searching for a dry pyjama top in a drawer in the dark. On a night like that she'd perspire as much as she would during a 45-minute run in the park. Her sweat would have a light smell of curry, old butter, and chlorine.

They took a few pictures on a cell phone. Photos of a face outlined with a wet towel. Then they went to the lockers, and used the hairdryers to dry their hair and swimsuits. Synthetics dry in no time, hair takes all eternity. Petra went for a run. After a shower, she'd quickly get ready for tomorrow's lecture. At night she'd hear voices behind the door of her dorm room. In different languages and accents. A little bit of cigarette smoke from the kitchenette would come in under her door. The neon light in the hallway would hum. Flies and moths would beat against the light cover. Summer turned to autumn. Paris calmed down. She felt that the heavy summer air was gone. But once in a while it would come back in her dreams.

ANKA, LONDON

Muv Po Polsku!

'Muv po polsku!' a guy leaned over the desk and shouted into Anka's face. She could understand almost everything he said. It amounted to: 'Speak Polish! Stop pretending you're from here. I've got eyes and ears, you're one of us, so don't speak English with me, you hear??' The guy had been looking for work for weeks, he was living in a ground-floor apartment with a Czech construction worker Jan, a Czech cell phone repairman Pavel, and two women who were looking for work, Olya and Iga, from Poland. The two of them spent half of each day browsing the internet, looking at ads. They wrote down contact information, made dots on a torn-up map, and headed to town. Always together. They had made a pact that one wouldn't get a job without the other. Pavel always came home at the same time, shut himself in his room, cracked open a beer, and spent hours talking to his girlfriend on a hacked cell phone. Jan came home a little later, flipped through channels for a while, and then mixed a few Tesco value products in a pan. Everyone bought white-blue-and-red products, 'the colour of our flags', as Jan put it. To keep track of things, everything in the fridge had a name written on it. Pavel also drew a line on his milk bottle. He suspected that Jan was using his milk in his coffee.

It was all too familiar to Anka, because until recently she had lived with them. She had channel-surfed on the worn-out couch. She had cooked on the pan that had the non-stick layer scratched off, was starting to rust, and imparted a reddish tinge to all foods. She had flipped through the magazines that Olya and Iga bought to find out about British celebrities first-hand. 'I don't like Victoria Beckham!' Olya would say in Polish. 'I like David Beckham,' Iga would respond. Anka moved out when she found a job at the local employment agency. She had gone to inquire, and they immediately sat her down at the office. Things changed, all of a sudden she had papers and someone was willing to take a look at her diploma. Translated, signed, with an official seal. That was when Anka saw the Virgin Mary on a screen saver opening and closing her cloak to bless her. She had a 12-star halo over her head. No more biking from the train station with cash in her back-pack. Now she had her own coffee cup in the kitchenette, and from her desk in a warm, dry office, she helped match the supply and demand of jobs.

She helped the Pole, Jacek, with housing. He was com-pletely lost. It took him two days to find the employment agency. He had the street name right, but instead of going to the *street*, he went to the *road*. The road was on the other end of London. By the time he made it to the wrong place, he was completely beaten up by the bus rides. In three hours he would have been a long way from Warsaw. On the way to the mountains or the coast. In London he had only crossed a few zones in that amount of time. Buses were cheaper than the tube. He regretted not having made himself a sandwich for the road from the soft toast bread. In a Turkish food stand he pointed to a rotating skewer and got a large kebab, 'eat here', which meant on a plate. Those who couldn't speak a word of English and were afraid to boot, would pay a stupid sum of money for an impossible-to-eat portion of meat, and they'd have to leave the rest behind until they'd learn to ask for 'takeaway', and preferably without onion. 'How much did you spend? That's Tesco value products for a week if I'm splurging!' Jan would have said.

The next day Jacek made it to the right office. From across her desk Anka could smell the sweaty mixture of new-arrival fear and yesterday's onion. A moon-shaped Slavic face was looking at her with blue eyes and colourless eyelashes. The thought that crossed her mind was how many different forms of ugliness there were. It was different for Brits than for Poles. She called the former turkeys and the latter potatoes. The former looked red through a face without pigment, as if they were angry. The latter always seemed to be embarrassed. When she pointed to the field *address*, that he had left blank, Jacek said: 'I don't have an address.' So she called Jan, told him to stop looking for a roommate, and sent Jacek to her former address. Ever since then, Jacek thought that Anka would be his guardian angel. But when she couldn't find him a job for a few weeks, he became desperate. He wouldn't be able to pay that week's rent, and Jan would say: 'I hear they have a nice lawn at the Polish embassy, I'll lend you a tent.'

'Muv po polsku!' he shouted, as Anka tried to explain to him that without English they wouldn't even take him at a construction site, a warehouse, and definitely not at a cash register. 'And what do I need to say behind a cash register? I'll say "hello", scan the groceries, and then I'll ask "plastic or paper?" and give them a bag! You think I can't handle that if any fat Black woman can?' Anka understood almost everything he was saying. Her grandmother was from a border region, every summer she had gone to markets in Poland with her mother, and she had spent her winters in the Tatras teaching snowboarding to groups of Poles. The desperate command 'Muv po polsku!' brought her to tears. Her colleague from the next desk cleared Jacek out of the office; he shoved him into the line of people waiting outside the door, and shouted some threat at him in his South African English. Anka went to make herself tea in her cup with the slogan *Think Pink*. She sat down at her desk and tried to carry on as usual. Red veins were scribbled across the whites of her eyes, her voice trembled, and her Slavic accent became stronger. The words softly stuck together, she couldn't meter them correctly. She had to repeat every sentence. On the phone someone said angrily: 'Am I the fucking last British person on Earth??'

In the evening she opened her umbrella and walked out onto the street. A large Black woman sitting on the steps outside the building hissed at her: 'You Polish crap!' Anka didn't even look at her; she pulled the strings on her collar tight and buttoned up her jacket. She thought about how this rain was snow in the Tatras, and she was only going to be there a little longer, and then, thanks to her saved up pounds, she'd get to hit the slopes in her new gear. She worked during the year, and during ski season she taught Poles to snowboard. The London fog would soon take the shape of a snowboard, boots, over-alls, and goggles with coloured glass through which everything would look pink, even in the fog.

Tate Gallery Blues

'A routine is like the beads of a rosary. Only a heathen gets bored,' Anka's grandma used to say to her. After coming to London, Anka quickly tried to build new everydayness. It started when she opened the door to her apartment, took a breath of the air inside, and made the decision to get out of there as soon as possible. She put her suitcase and her handbag into her future room. There was nothing in it except a bed, a closet with no shelves, and a mirror with a stain next to it. The suitcase hit the floor, and the echo in the empty space returned the thud. After that, only the TV could be heard, as Olya and Iga tried to understand *British Idol*. Anka introduced herself to everyone. In between setting down her suitcase and tomorrow's job search was a space she didn't know how to fill. Until then everything had been more or less clear. Now she faced a stain on the wall, grey sheets, and a ton of free time.

She knocked on Pavel's door. Their rooms were next to each other, and an endless muted conversation between London and Ostrava was coming through under the threshold. And the smell of cigarettes. Anka asked him for one and went to sit outside. On a bench with a view of the highway. It may have been the last house in London. Zone 6; beyond it were only trees, fences, and roads. Anka thought she saw a black horse ride by with a gentleman in a cape on it.

'The first time I came home after six months, I wanted to have the word BUNS tattooed in gothic script on my deflated stomach,' Jan said once when they were sitting on the bench together, drinking beer out of cans. 'I listened to Landa, hated Blacks, Brits, Pakistanis, and loved my mom. Then I came home, gorged myself on buns, and had to fly back because I didn't get time off. I still had powdered sugar on my mouth when the plane was taking off.' Anka thought that Jan's stories were embarrassing, but after what he said about the buns, she put her arm around his shoulders. They clinked cans. After two more, Jan blurted out his desperate desire to caress her bun. Anka tossed her cigarette, patted him on the head, and went back to the room with a stain on the wall. The next day she found a different place to live on the internet, and within a week she moved. Closer to work. Further away from beer cans and thoughts of mom. The night Anka was packing, Jan played Landa's music really loud and then he called his mother on Pavel's phone with endless minutes.

On the way to her new apartment she got drenched. She threw her suitcase and her bag on the floor. The water that drained off the suitcase made a stain on the wall. That was the last desperate gesture, she promised herself. *Think Pink*! The next day she didn't go straight to the apartment after work, instead she crossed the bridge to the new Tate Gallery. 'Most museums are free here. Go check it out, I've already seen them all,' Jan told her on the bench. The large industrial building had unlimited space for Anka's free time. She walked from floor to floor, read all the exhibit labels, had coffee, and went back the next day. When she ran out of exhibits, she went to a different gallery. She knew that if she didn't go there, she'd be going to a room with a stain and roommates who grilled hot dogs in a shopping cart on Sundays.

She wrote herself messages on the paper sleeves that protect your hand from hot coffee, and she hung them on a board above her desk at the office. *I love challenges! Think outside the box! Just keep on keeping on! Step by step and smile (if possible).* She also collected postcards and various flyers to put them on the wall in her room. Event invitations, club flyers, and artists' cards. They covered the stain on the wall and dampened the echo. She even considered going to a football match with her colleagues at the end of the week, to find out whether she liked Beckham or not.

Why It's Good to Have an Oyster Card

It may seem that Anka could have done all sorts of things in London. She didn't have to avoid cookouts in the courtyard or buy Tesco value products. One day she told herself that very thing. Instead of going to the Tate Gallery, she went to Sainsbury and bought really good hot dogs. She had made up her mind that she'd stand in the checkout lane and be—in a better supermarket where the cashiers weren't Black women with an odd number of fake nails, where real Brits shopped, freckled and in striped suits—be happy. She wouldn't have that tightness in her lungs because of trying to save as much as possible. Cooking out was nothing special. Firewood was sold in bundles at gas stations and in supermarkets. Little houses with a strip of a garden were equipped for cookouts. It wasn't as though someone had designed a house for a grill to stand out. A grill was just part of it. A grill was part and parcel even for immigrants from South Africa like Anka's new roommates. In a Victorian house in East London, where the buildings didn't follow the basic principle of Feng Shui and their stairwells pointed to the door so that not a pound would stay in the house, she had a room on the ground floor of one such small house. Having a ground floor room was a step up, because there was another room in the basement, which had no windows and nothing ever dried in it. The rest of the rooms were occupied by South Africans who spoke funny English and even funnier Dutch. They were white as if they had come from a mill. The men had lime-covered boots in front of their doors, and the women had several white uniform blouses hanging in their closets. All of them ate frozen products, and everyone had his own shelf in the fridge. Each person had a laundry day. Outside in the yard there was a clothesline, standing there like a burnt tree, lifting its arms to the sky in vain, because there was a dryer above the washer. The tenants sat under the clothesline on plastic chairs, smoked, and put out the cigarette butts in the grass.

A little further, pavers lead to a tiled area with a Tesco cart. The cart served as a grill. Anka set her Sainsbury hot dogs next to her roommates' sausages and steaks. She had decided to share her elegantly pale, spiced hot dogs with them. It happened sometime between making the offer and going to switch her laundry from the washer to the dryer. In any case, she ended up with Tesco value hot dogs on her plate, and never found out what Sainsbury hot dogs taste like.

The next day she stood under the large sculpture in the entrance hall of the Tate Gallery. She no longer knew the difference between how good and bad people behaved, her intuition wasn't working, so she stood there looking and looking, and she couldn't do anything but hope that she'd get used to it, because everyone at home had told her that things would get better once she looked around and got used to it.

She'd have an easier time getting used to it over a familiar beer. It was a Czech beer, we should add in a whisper. She was sitting in a Czechoslovak pub and hoping that things would become clear again, that bad people would be bad and the good be good. She needed to separate them with a road full of unpredictable island traffic. Look left! Look right! But by then the word had spread over the tables that she was saving up for snowboarding gear, that she had found an office job and moved, that she had bought herself Sainsbury hot dogs and drank coffee at the museum, that she had her own cup at the office, and that they grilled on the weekends. She was sitting at a table with a chequered washable tablecloth, and her countrymen were asking her how and where she had found the job, if they had any other openings, if another bed wouldn't fit in her room, if they needed someone to do house cleaning, if she didn't have a few hot dogs left, and if she had some original CD they could copy, because everyone had run out of things to listen to. Preferably something Slovak or Czech, something where they sang about love and had heavy metal guitars.

She rode the free bus from East London to the centre and back with people from her neighbourhood. On the way she fell asleep from exhaustion, and when she woke up, there was a Pakistani mother sitting by her feet, nursing with her eyes closed, a Chinese man dozing, leaning against a cart with wrapped T-shirts, a large Black man with an arm outstretched as if he were shooting at a basket who had fallen asleep before he had grabbed onto the handrail, and two South Africans leaning against one another with their lime-covered boots and splattered foreheads, asleep. Everyone was sleeping. Anka woke up in a slightly different *National Geographic*, the one printed on glossy paper in which a little Black kid is jumping high, a smiling Chinese woman is carrying a basket on her head, and an Eskimo is carrying a large fish. She felt embarrassed to be taking the bus with people who had travelled great distances only to push wheelbarrows and slam cash register drawers. Because there was no other way, in fact, this was better. After all, she was saving up for snowboarding gear! She bought herself an Oyster card and started to ride the Underground. From then on, all she saw was her house, her office, and museums. Everything else disappeared mercifully in the Underground. It made her day much simpler. She'd call home and say she was doing fine. She was doing great.

Krištof and Krištof

A pair of white boots was sitting by the door to Anka's room. Another pair of work boots covered in a layer of lime dust stood by the next room. But those were there every night, they disappeared early in the morning, and came back in the afternoon. A different pair of such boots was now in front of Anka's room. Before asking whom they belonged to, she peered into the room. Closed curtains made the room dark. She didn't normally close the curtains. Her bed had been shoved under the window, and there was a new daybed by the door. The covers were rising and falling, a man was sleeping there, a labourer judging by the shoes, a medium-sized White man, he could have been an Englishman in light of his freckles, but why would a local push a wheelbarrow at a construction site and live on the ground floor of a Victorian cottage in East London? Anka closed the door and took her questions to the courtyard.

Martina was sitting in the courtyard, smoking a rolled cigarette in her yellow cleaning gloves. Once a month the whole house chipped in for Martina. She came, put on her gloves, washed the bathroom, the toilet, and the kitchen, vacuumed the floors, and smoked a few cigarettes with the tenants. No one had such an egalitarian disposition towards a cleaning woman as the people at this house. Rather than squabbling over who should clean what and when, they instituted a fee for Martina, and she added them to the list of the houses she cleaned.

'The landlord moved him into your room,' Martina said before Anka had a chance to ask. She handed Anka a packet of tobacco so she'd roll a cigarette for each of them. Anka protested, saying she didn't roll that well. 'I'm supposed to roll myself in gloves?' Martina spoke with a heavy Hungarian accent and compensated for it by inserting reflexive pronouns everywhere. What she knew about the sleeping man was that the bed had shown up first. The landlord walked through the house from top to bottom, and since everyone was at home, they defended their rooms. Anka ended up with the bed in her room and with freckled James. Then the guilty inhabitants of the house made themselves scarce. 'All of themselves went out for a beer.' Once in a while the roommates went with some of their countrymen to the South African pub on the corner. This was their neighbourhood. James was from New Zealand; no one knew where he had come from or where he was going. All of a sudden he was sleeping in a cottage in East London and working at a nearby construction site.

Martina picked up the cigarette butts from the devastated lawn. The two of them sat on plastic chairs under the clothes line, thinking about what to do with the man in Anka's room. 'Ask them to lower your rent,' Martina suggested. 'At least if he were good-looking . . .' she kept musing. 'At our house we have an empty room, what do you call it, the one that's underground. But the landlord doesn't want to rent it. You could ask if himself would put him there.'

Before James woke up, Anka and Martina went to look at the basement room. The door under the stairwell was swollen from humidity. The room had no windows and it was being used for storage, but there was still a king-size bed in the middle of it. 'At the beginning I lived here with my boyfriend.' Anka couldn't imagine how one could breathe, let alone live there. 'You get used to it. But my clothes always smelt bad.' After two months, her boyfriend had had enough of London. Instead of getting to see the big world, they were sitting in a courtyard with a trampled brown lawn; a week later they had to switch from Marlboros to a packet of Drum, and then to even cheaper tobacco. They spent the first few weeks looking for work together. Then Martina inherited a list of houses from a girl who had to go home on short notice. It was like winning the lottery. She didn't have to say a word in English all day. The other girl introduced her to the homeowners, and then Martina was left alone with cleaning products and a vacuum. In the evenings her boyfriend was waiting for her in the courtyard, grilling Tesco knockwursts, and sadly watching the passing clouds. 'Why don't you take a walk somewhere?' Martina would ask him at first. 'Where should I go?' he snapped. Going out for a beer after work was a thing of the past. It was an unnecessary luxury. Instead they bought cans like everyone else and tossed them around the grill. They visited every museum the first week. Once in a while they went for a picnic at a park. All of the parks were the same. Nightclubs were expensive, and throngs of dressed up teenagers stood in front of them. No sneakers, long trousers.

Martina's boyfriend's name was Krištof, a Slovak version of Christopher, but his passion for exploration was short lived. A low-cost flight had dropped them off at Stansted Airport. A bus drove them through town, where everything seemed small, like a miniature of European cities. A lot of brick walls, flowers, greenery . . . like a village, Krištof thought. And towering over it, Big Ben and the Parliament building, which looked like the one in Budapest to Krištof, except smaller. The walks started out in style. They crisscrossed the centre of town. They took pictures under statues of generals and queens. Martina made sandwiches on soft bread for their outings, and they ate them on park benches. Once she started to work, she left the walking to Krištof. In the morning she made a sandwich for each of them, and then they went their separate ways. Krištof got on the free bus to the centre of London. He kept going to more and more remote streets, discovering less and less. He sat in a park. He smoked on a square. He filled his water bottle at a museum.

One morning he was lying in the stale basement room, wondering what the weather was like outside. The room had no windows, so there was no view of the sky. Yesterday's clothes were still wet on the drying rack. Martina got up, took the wet things, and put them in the dryer; she made sandwiches, had a cigarette and coffee with one of the women from the house, they exchanged very few words in English, but somehow they understood one another. Krištof was standing in the courtyard, looking at the sky. He wished for endless rain so that he wouldn't have to walk around town. But the sky had been clear for almost a week. He sat on a worn out plastic chair and watched the sky. That afternoon it started to rain. In the evening he told Martina that he had summoned the rain. Martina told him that he had rounded the bend, and he should really do something with himself. But Krištof didn't want to go for a walk. All those walks made him feel like he was in therapy. He crumbled the sandwich for the ants and the birds in the courtyard. Martina didn't come home that evening. Her roommate took her to a South African bar, and Martina caught the bartender's eye. 'Go to the bar, he wants to buy you a drink. He's in love with you,' her roommate said to her. 'He loves you. You can choose a drink! Go for it, girl!' She could pick whatever she wanted. His treat. She pointed to the colourful bottles in the fridge. She didn't know which one to choose. 'I'd say raspberry for you!' He handed her a frosty red bottle. When she came home, Krištof said he knew. 'I had the feeling that you were somewhere with someone,' he said. 'Jesus, I must be somewhere with someone if I'm not here! I don't need to stare at the sky for an hour to come up with that!'

In East London, in a South African bar, while drinking a raspberry cooler, Martina started to put together a different version of her relationship with Krištof. The big shot in Komárno was a big baby in London. At home he had his hands in Škoda engines all day at his father's car repair shop, he had a spoonful of goulash in his mouth from his mother's restaurant, his pockets were filled with sausages and cakes from his grandma, Martina cut his hair, his friends patted him on the back, they passed around a joint and clinked beer mugs. Martina noticed that Krištof was losing a lot of weight.

He didn't buy groceries; he must have only been eating the one sandwich a day and cornflakes out of the box with Martina's name on it. The only thing he bought was tobacco.

When they went to bed at night and turned out the lights, the room was completely dark. The damp air reminded her of a summerhouse after a long winter—wet covers and a hunch about a dead mouse. She noticed that Krištof's eyes were open. 'Why aren't you sleeping?' He said he wasn't tired. 'Why should I be tired?' 'From doing nothing,' Martina snapped, and she turned to her side so as not to see him. He exhaled nicotine-laden air. She asked: 'Do you want to go home?' He was asleep. He didn't say a word. Maybe he wasn't asleep. He didn't say a word. When Martina moved in with the bartender, it was supposed to be temporary. She was crying at the bar with colourful cooler bottles in front of her. She got drunk, stayed past closing time, and they sat on the bar. She cobbled together Esperanto out of English, Hungarian, and Slovak. She spent the night at his place, in a room above the establishment, up a narrow staircase. In the morning she said 'yuck' about her own T-shirt, which had salty rings under the armpits, and laughed it off: 'Stress.' She put on deodorant, got dressed, and went to work. At the door she turned around, kissed him on the cheek, and they had a cigarette together in the window facing the street. Krištof was walking down that street, without a sandwich, he was going to get tobacco, or was just out for a walk.

He didn't get far, Martina found him sitting on a cardboard box a short distance from the house. It was evening. He sat there waiting for rain. He wanted to catch cold and die. He recalled a poem they used to laugh about when they were little, and how funny Martina sounded reciting it with a Hungarian accent:

A falcon took flight
It was raining that night
It got wet and died.

She entertained the whole class by reading Štúr's poetry in her Hungarian Slovak. The teacher, who enunciated and softened every word so much that the classroom smelt of bread and linden, kept cringing. The children laughed so hard that they beat their desks and squealed. Krištof carved a heart on her desk with his compass.

She pulled him by the hand, but he couldn't get up. He had bought himself a box of wine, and arranged everything to make it look exactly the way he felt. Like a loser, who had come to London to make a fool of himself. To walk around eight hours a day, not to have enough money for a decent meal, not to be able to go have a beer with friends, to smoke dried bird droppings, to let his roommates act like he's not in the room, he had heard them say that he's a 'freak'. He couldn't get up off the cardboard. 'Did you pee yourself?' Martina asked, but it was probably just spilt wine. She stepped on his feet and tried to get him up. When his butt was off the ground, he shoved her aside and she fell to the ground; he thrashed his feet trying to kick her, aiming for her neck where she had a red hickey. Martina quickly got up. She ran off, but came back immediately, threw the wine box in a dustbin, took him by the hand, and dragged him away from the cardboard box. 'Stop staring, you moron!' she shouted through tears at a passer-by, who crossed to the other side of the street. 'Let's go home,' Krištof finally said. Martina kept dragging him, lifting him, rolling him over, she wanted to take him home, but a room with no windows wasn't the 'home' he was talking about.

He spent a few more days lying on the bed in the room. He didn't even turn the lights on, he put a box of wine under the bed, his sandwich fell to the ground as he was groping for his watch. He hoped that after Martina finished cleaning, she'd come there. She came back two days later, packed his things, and said that she had bought him a low-cost flight, and that he should go to Stansted the next day. Once again the bus ride, brick walls, glass city, crowded Oxford Street, parks, hanging geraniums. She offered to go with him to the airport, but she probably just wanted to make sure that he left. The bartender wanted to go with her, to carry the suitcases. She refused. 'He'd see who I've been living with!' Martina said to Anka. She dampened Anka's hair and started to cut it. Then her landlord moved her to the room upstairs. He stopped renting the basement room. Martina wanted to fix it up for cutting hair, set up a little salon. There was a bathroom and a large mirror. But the landlord didn't like the idea. He said that she had a room and should stop bothering him, and wouldn't she like to move in with her new boyfriend. 'I'll move in, and when we break up, he'll kick me out to the curb. I'll end up sitting on cardboard, right?' She was practical about it. She cut hair in her bathroom, or in people's homes. She cut her bartender's hair too. She cut the hair of everyone in the house, then their colleagues' hair, and the South African blond neighbours' hair. She didn't take walks. There was no time. The circle where she cleaned, cut hair, and went out for beer was smaller than Komárno. It was practically a village. Nothing but short Victorian cottages.

Martina swept up the hair. Anka came to terms with the idea that she'd sleep next to freckled James that night. The next day she'd call Martina's landlord and ask him whether he wouldn't rent the basement room to a guy from New Zealand. If not, she'd call her own landlord and ask to have her rent split in half with James. 'We must our own rights!' Martina said as she dumped the hair into a dustbin. Anka wondered what her parents would say if she told them on the phone that she was sleeping in a room with a construction worker. They would not picture James as a naked freckled shoulder rising and falling during sleep, pulled curtains, and white boots set in front of the door. James looked more like a backpacker who was on a trip across Europe with two T-shirts and a raincoat. A construction worker . . . Her parents would have imagined a man with fists like hammers, yellowed fingernails, a tanned back, and sweaty overalls. A man who drank beer before work and liquor after. Alcohol wafting from him on public transportation and women with bags moving to a different seat. Anka changed in a locked bathroom and slipped under the covers. James stirred and said, 'Hi, let's talk in the morning! I'm really tired now.' Then he stirred again. 'By the way, I'm James.'

After the freckled shoulder spoke with a heavy accent, she couldn't send the person to live in a mouldy basement in Martina's house. The shoulder spoke, early in the morning it took its boots, and went to a construction site. In the afternoon it read Terry Pratchett and laughed out loud. Not long after, it went to Europe, to the continent. That's how James referred to it—the islands and the continent. A New Zealander's perspective. The ocean was the important thing. James disappeared the same way he had appeared. Only some lime dust remained in front of the door. He didn't settle down, didn't get involved with anyone, in a romance or a fight, he didn't borrow anything, didn't leave anything behind, he disappeared before the inhabitants of the house could develop an opinion of him, he was gone, gone with the wind that blew towards the sea. A true Christopher Columbus. 'We landlocked people are so sad and fettered . . .' Anka said to Martina as they smoked. They were sitting in the courtyard, smoking, and looking at the clouds floating across the sky. It was about to rain.

The Moon in Foil

Anka invited her mother to inspect her new living arrangements. She finally had something to show her. A small apartment she was renting with Martina. She waited for her mother at the airport, took her by the hand, and led her through the centre of London. She made her tea with milk and bought her a lamb kebab. She took a picture of her with Robert Redford at Madame Tussauds. She sat her down in the grass at a park and took off her shoes so that she could experience the velvety greenery. How those bushy colourful geraniums hanging from lampposts and pub walls got watered, she couldn't say. She showed her how Tower Bridge opened so that boats could float underneath it. They listened to Big Ben. She set her up in her own bed, and went to sleep on the living room couch. In the middle of the night her mother woke her up, asking to sleep on the couch. 'I can't sleep on something that soft,' she whispered into the darkness. In the morning Anka found her mom making breakfast for her and Martina.

Mom refused to go out for sushi. Whenever Anka came to visit, she packed the fridge with things her mom didn't know how to use and said they always just went bad. A lot of pretty packages with English labels. Her mom knew a little bit of Russian, a few words in German, and she could get along well in Polish. One time she had spent a whole month creaming herself with a nice smelling pearlescent shower gel, thinking it was a body lotion. Her dermatologist told her to take a shower and gave her pills to calm down the allergic reaction.

Anka watched her mother's eyelashes as she blinked while converting pounds to crowns and then to euros. In a restaurant where Anka took her for dinner, she asked for an English breakfast. She made her choices based on the column on the right. 'Mom, order whatever you like!' She kept persuading Anka that what she really wanted was a sausage, sunny side up, tomato, and white beans. Then she spent the whole night making herself black tea for her irritated gallbladder. 'Anka, I'm so glad that I didn't leave in '68! I could never get used to living here.'

'Some people are like that, you could pull down the moon, wrap it in foil, and bake it for them, but all they want is plain bread.' Anka laughed at the unusual comparison. Perhaps it made more sense in Finnish. In Slovak it sounded strange.

It was also strange when a girl sitting next to Anka took a look at her passport, opened her mouth, and the translucent Scandinavian face said something in Slovak. Her fellow traveller was explaining her theory of the connection between the body and mind. Our facial muscles take on their shape based on how we use them in our native language. When we learn another language, our face changes. The muscles gently add new layers, new ligaments stand out around the mouth, the corners of the mouth move in new ways, we breathe differently between words, and we blink differently. Thus when people who have lived abroad for a long time come back, their faces look different. Anka thought that her father must look completely different by now. Talking and looking like a foreigner. Since '68.

The Finnish girl Riina had spent a lot of time speaking Russian. Her souvenir from Petrograd was an ability to talk about problems and worries. Even with a fellow passenger on a plane. 'I offered him Russian palaces and then a view from the Statue of Liberty, but he wanted to stay home. He said he was used to Helsinki, and he wasn't going to wash dishes in America. So I told him to stay and wait for the moths to hatch in his closet. Then he'll really feel at home.' She was talking about her Slovak boyfriend. Anka talked about her mother, who had spent the rest of her time in London washing dishes, vacuuming, and window washing. She looked out onto the street through the clean windows and was surprised to see a different town. When Anka came home from work, her mother always told her what she had seen through the window. 'That neighbour keeps bringing home a man. They don't even close the curtains. And the lady across from you has those bushy geraniums. Would you ask her if she pours meat juice on them to get them to bloom so well?'

Anka got on the bus from Stansted. Without even dropping off her suitcases, she made an appointment at a tattoo parlour that she passed by every day on her way to work. She showed a word printed in letters that looked like they came from her grandmother's Bible to the slight Japanese woman who worked there. The Japanese woman looked at the gothic script for a while, and then she read BUNS. She raised her eyebrows, a thin tattooed line that transformed her into

Marlene Dietrich. 'Beautiful!' she said and started to draw the letters on Anka's stomach. The first jabs hurt so much that Anka wanted to jump up, run down the street in her underwear, and not stop until the last zone, beyond which are only trees, fences, and roads. Then the sensation changed. The pain kept twisting until it took on a strange form. It turned sweet. Instead of droplets of blood, her belly looked like it had been dusted with powdered sugar. She had gotten used to it.

MIKA, HELSINKI

A Fur Coat in Helsinki

'Would you like to take a fur coat with you? It's got to be thirty below zero there!' His mother opened the closet, pushed aside a moth glue trap with her finger, and pulled out a heavy ram fur coat. Michal was eating a thick beef broth, but the smell of mothballs forced him to put down his spoon and turn towards his mother. She was standing in the hallway and made him try on a multigenerational fur coat. 'Your grandfather got it from his father, who was a tanner. No one in the family ever had to buy a fur coat. He made a custom fur coat for everyone, and all of them are good to this day!'

Wearing the fur coat, Michal felt like an advertisement for vodka. 'Mom, only Russians wear fur coats in Helsinki in wintertime!' No one wanted to look like a Russian in Helsinki. Not in the winter, nor in the summer. When he took a ferry to Tallinn, Estonia, with his colleagues from work, they warned him that Russian taxi drivers would be waiting at the harbour, and when they'd see someone flag a taxi, they'd zip ahead of the official taxi company and illegally pick up the ride. 'So what's the problem?' asked Michal. 'That they're doing it illegally! They don't pay taxes. They're disrupting the system!' his Finnish colleagues explained. Michal had noticed that even when his colleagues were drunk, they always stood on the right on escalators, so as not to disrupt the system. If they got so drunk that they could no longer move, they'd just make it outside the pub, fall into a snowdrift, and a service would come pick them up and take them home, because the system was working.

A Turkish colleague added that in Turkey no one wanted to be *White* any more because of the Russians. Russian prostitutes undersold themselves. 'A Russian woman will do what our prostitutes wouldn't be willing to!' A fur coat in Helsinki would be an albatross for an immigrant with a Russian sounding name like Michal. 'Maybe you should change your name,' his Turkish colleague suggested. 'Do you have a middle name?' he asked. 'Samuel, after my grandfather,' Michal said. 'Not good, not good! Sounds Jewish.' So Michal started to use the Finnish version of his name, Mika. His Turkish colleague might have been happy with it, had he not seen a Mika in tight jeans and with effeminate gestures on MTV.

'Grandpa made it all the way to America with his craft. When he was walking around Nový York, as he called it, he heard a voice from the sky: "Samko, Samko!" Grandpa got scared, but then he said to himself that he was righteous, so he had nothing to fear. And he kept going. "Samko, Samko!" the voice kept calling. He looked up, and there, on the 135th floor, Zuza from back home was hanging out of a window and waving at him. And he said, "What are you doing up there, Zuza, you'll fall, get down from there!" And she said,

"I'm washing the windows!" ' His mother helped Mika take off the fur coat and started to sew on a button that was hanging by a thread. 'And then grandpa came back, and he and grandma Zuza built the biggest house far and wide!' Whenever Mika visited, his mother recalled family stories. 'Mom, I'm not taking that fur coat with me, and you should consider throwing it out. The whole house smells of mothballs!' His mother kept sewing the button on with a cobbler's needle that could get through ram's skin. 'I used to buy moth traps, but ever since the housewares store around the corner closed, I've not been able to find them anywhere. Mothballs and lavender are best anyway. Grandpa used to put them into fur coats as well. The mothball smell airs out quickly in freezing air.'

Mika served himself the main course, thick spätzle that barely came off the spoon, and hid the strudel in the pantry so that his mother wouldn't offer him any. A moth flew out of the pantry and landed on his T-shirt that said 'Welcome to Helsinki.' Michal swatted it. 'Mom, why do you have enough supplies in that pantry again as if World War III were about to break out?? I told you to buy only what you can eat, and stop lugging home full bags like rustics!' His mother tore the end of the thread with her teeth and through the corner of her mouth she said: 'OK, Miško. Keep educating us. Grandpa also had a progressive household when he came back. Everyone looked over his fence and said: "Look at what the American's doing!" '

Northern Lights

On Friday evening cars kept circling outside the supermarket, looking for a parking spot. On Friday evening customers kept circling inside the supermarket, filling their carts with cartons of beer. Liquor stores were already closed. The supermarkets only sold beer. Mika thought that the little bottles of beer looked as though no one in the entire country was old enough to drink alcohol.

He and his colleagues were supplying themselves for Friday night. They finished the beer in the car, and then they went to a bar. His Turkish colleague explained the rules of drinking to him. Drink quickly and mix. Down. To the dance floor. In front of the karaoke screen. Then he invited him to get some air. He blew smoke rings and looked at the sky. 'If the power went out, we'd see the northern lights,' he said. 'The northern lights increase your libido. People don't act like themselves. Not only do Finns have the best school system in Europe, they also lead in sexual activity charts.' When they finished smoking, his Turkish colleague took him by the arm. 'Come, Mika, let's find someone and try out the northern lights. Finnish women are feminists. They drag you to bed themselves.'

Mika looked around the dance floor, checking out the dancing women. They didn't look like feminists. He wasn't sure what he should be looking for. He asked his Turkish colleague how he knew that they were feminists. 'If things were left up to the men here, they'd die out. Women have taken over the decision making. They choose. Watch them!' Mika kept looking at the dance floor. Everything looked as it would at a regular club. The men had vacant stares and the women had sweat soaked tank tops. When a female colleague he hadn't noticed before approached him, he was glad he could stop searching for feminists and thinking about the northern lights. He bought her a drink and let her buy him the next one. After the second drink she started to speak Russian. Without an accent. 'You're Russian? Your Finnish is excellent! I'm afraid I'll never learn it that well.' He talked about Finnish and Hungarian, the outlier languages that supposedly only have 20 words in common, so they're not mutually understandable. They tried to figure out the 20 words. They started with things such as water, horse, sun, love.

She said she had spent two years studying in Russia. Mika realized that all he remembered in Russian was an off-key *Minja zavut* and the names of a couple of fruits from when they had to play store. Then mandatory Russian was dropped. Instead they could choose between *Ich heisse* and *My name is*. He thought it funny how everyone assumed that Slovaks had one foot in Russia. He knew nothing about Russia, except for the names of a few authors he hadn't read. His Finnish colleague spoke Russian without an accent, knew contemporary Russian music, and had a lot of stories from dorms, trains, and markets. She had seen the museums and read the books. Mika dared to formulate the thought that the current cultural blockade was in the East. 'The curtain simply shifted,' she said.

After this sentence it would have been awkward to invite Riina to the dance floor where their Turkish colleague was lifting a young woman's spaghetti straps while dancing with her. Instead Mika invited her outside. 'If all the lights in the city went out, we might see the northern lights,' he said. 'Rubbish. We'd have to travel further north,' she said. Perhaps under the influence of a strong magnetic field, he asked: 'Are you a feminist?' His colleague laughed. 'You're funny, I like you,' she said and kissed him. A sticky kiss from the black asphalt drink called salmiakki.

You Can Be Not Afraid

'You can be not afraid!' Riina said to Mika and squeezed his cold hand on the armrest. There was whiteness outside the round airplane window. 'You don't have to be afraid,' he corrected her. Riina had switched from Russian to Slovak in record time. He could hardly believe it. As they talked, she asked him about vocabulary, sentences, grammar, and exceptions. And suddenly she was speaking with him in broken Slovak.

Riina's first visit at Mika's was like he had brought home a magical talking machine from up north. 'She speaks!' his little cousin shouted while running around the couch. 'Her name is Riina,' he admonished his cousin quietly. She hung on Riina's neck, demanded attention, squealed, recited, and kept lifting her skirt to show off what was written on her underwear. 'Thursday,' the talking doll read. 'But today is Tuesday!' Riina said, and the cousin squealed as if the underwear itself had spoken, and then ran to her mother.

On the plane he wondered what it would be like to introduce Riina at home. To sit her down at the table, to leave her alone in the room with her parents for a moment, to take her to go out with his friends. His father pulled out Riina's chair and seated her, old style. His mother lifted up the pot lid to show off what she had prepared for them. 'Is it borsch?' Riina asked when she dipped her spoon into the pleasant-smelling cabbage soup. 'I was always under the impression that Finns and Russians didn't like each other,' his father said. He always considered visiting foreigners a source for verifying information about international politics. The only people he hadn't bothered with politics were the exhausted frightened Americans, the Kosowskis.

Right after the revolution, Mr. Kosowski came to teach at the school where Michal's father worked. Inspired by his last name, Mr. Kosowski was quite sentimental about this region, by which he meant the part of Europe between the Adriatic and the Baltic seas. His wife, however, must have been reading different Beadekers. Michal's father could still remember the look in her eyes. When Mrs. Kosowski opened one of their many oversized suitcases, it all made sense. She had brought everything. Everything, packed to go to a country that was supposed to have nothing. Toilet paper, coat hangers, medicines, cosmetics, extra shoe laces, paper toilet-seat covers . . .

The Kosowskis had come to Michal's parents' house straight from the airport, each of them holding a small child, both of which had gotten sick during the trip. The younger child was asleep, the older was picking its nose and had a vacant expression. Mrs. Kosowski's eyes blinked rapidly. She kept watching Michal's mother's hands as she made tea for the children, and kept repeating a very loud, enunciated 'Thank you.' In this situation of fear and panic, when the Kosowskis barely ate a few pretzel sticks and snuck paper seat covers to the toilet, Michal's father decided not to ask any questions. 'They think that communism was like the bubonic plague, and that it's still in the air,' he said after they had taken the Kosowskis to the best hotel in town. 'Mrs. Kosowski has a suitcase full of nothing but cleaning products,' his mother said. 'I had to boil the water for tea twice! Who has ever seen such a thing? What are we, savages? Yet she let her kid eat pretzel sticks with fingers that had been up its nose the whole time!'

Mika held Riina's hand under the table. His cousin stood right next to her and carefully watched Riina's face. That was when he noticed the blue veins that were visible under her Scandinavian skin. That night, when they lay down on the made-up sofa, he observed how visible her circulatory system was throughout her body. He asked her to lift her pyjama top, and his finger followed the blue trails up to her heart. It would have never occurred to him in Helsinki. There was nothing unusual about her body or face there. She was a Finnish woman of average beauty, and she was unusually talkative and open. 'They should send you to schools as a teaching aid,' he said with his finger on a vein. 'You racist! You don't like White people!' Riina laughed. 'You're not white! You're transparent!' His cousin called her the Snow Queen.

Riina unwrapped a cookbook. A giant cookbook that was supposed to be the start of a future of Riina and Mika as a couple. It was his mother's way of giving them her blessing in 365 pages. Riina winked at Mika: 'From now on I belong in the kitchen!' His father was also looking to connect. He poured Riina a small shot of slivovica and told her that he had corresponded with a Finnish woman for a few years. 'All those years I wrote to her about hockey, because I played back then. After two years she suggested that we exchange photographs. So I got my picture taken in my gear and sent it. When her photo arrived, I nearly fell over!' 'Was she very beautiful?' Riina asked, her eyes shiny from the alcohol. 'She was a girl! The whole time I thought I was writing to a boy, a buddy!' Riina burst out laughing. 'Did you visit her?' she asked. 'Oh no! I got scared. And I was embarrassed for bothering her for so long with things she wasn't interested in.' Riina disagreed: 'Maybe she was interested. In hockey, I mean. And in you, too!'

His father refilled the shot glasses, and his mother set grandma's strudel, the pride of their house, on the table. 'You know what?' Riina said, her eyes gleaming. 'You write her again, and Mika and I will go visit her if she writes you back. This is so exciting! I like it!' But his father had lost the address. 'You don't want to look for her!' Riina said, laughing. He swore that he had lost it back when he was still living with his parents. All of the letters were gone, he couldn't even remember her name. It was a name that could work for a boy or a girl. Probably ended with an *a*. Riina came up with a few names, but his father just laughed. Each of them reminded him of the hockey expert from years ago.

She fell asleep on the couch after having to count to 10 over and over again, strudel in hand. Mika's cousin was learning Finnish numbers: yksi, kaksi, kolme, neljä, viisi, kuusi . . . 'I thought they'd be similar to Hungarian,' his father said. Riina fell asleep, and the cousin pointed at objects all around, enchanting them with Finnish numbers. Mika's mother covered her with a blanket and quietly cleared the table. Riina was lying on the couch, worn out by the new environment like the sick Kosowski children. Mika caressed her translucent cheek and was no longer worried about her.

Rid of Her!

His body developed a strange habit. He'd wake up before the garbage collectors started to make noise outside, and then he'd toss and turn for a long time before falling back asleep. It went on for weeks. He told his Turkish colleague about it at lunch, and the colleague suggested that he go see a psychologist— the company would pay for it. Mika said that he felt embarrassed. It made him feel like a total wreck. True, He kept waking up in a sweat with his heart racing, and it took him an hour to get back to normal. Nevertheless, he didn't feel ripe for a psychologist. After all, he wasn't opening his coat in front of children at a park, nor was he running around the company office with a knife. He was just waking up in the wee hours. 'People aren't embarrassed to see a psychologist here. It's completely normal. What's not normal is bothering your friends with it. Of course, you're not bothering me,' Çem said. 'Find a male psychologist if you're embarrassed to cry in front of a woman. Tell him that your girlfriend left and it's hard on you.'

After Çem's analysis Mika didn't need to go see a psychologist. Çem hit the nail on the head. That was it. She hadn't left him, she just went back to study in Russia. Now they saw each other once every month or two, sometimes less. She had left the company's 'open space' and went to study Russian literature. She said she was following her dreams. With her roommates she went shopping at the big market.

They cooked together, everyone made what he or she knew with whatever ingredients were available. They ate pickles straight out of the jar, drank vodka from mustard glasses, and talked about literature in the kitchen until all hours. They were renting a fantastic apartment, as big as the whole office in Helsinki. With a disproportionately small bathroom that was separated from the kitchen only by a curtain. The tall windows opened onto the square right in the middle of Saint Petersburg. Everything was huge there. Building facades looked as though they were marching and celebrating. Riina spent eight hours a day in a library full of gold and rare wood.

While Mika had white iPod cables coming out of his ears as he was learning another programming language, Riina was hunched over well-worn books, taking notes. It was remarkable how thick a book she could read over the weekend whenever she came back. He was impressed. She called it speed reading. As if she weren't reading the lines left to right, but down the middle. He had no idea how. However she did it, she read that way on the plane from Saint Petersburg, on the bus and on the metro, at the table as well as in bed. He opened his eyes thinking that the garbage truck had woken him, and he tossed and turned under the covers. He went into the bathroom, got some water, and lay back down. The bed was uncomfortable. He was lying straight, but the surface seemed to be tilting. He kept moving around to balance the unevenness. By the time he got comfortable enough to close his eyes for a little while, he heard the sound of glass. It sounded as though he had toppled the glass of water he had set by the bed. But it was the alarm. He'd have to change the ringtone, it was an awful sound. Morning sounds are too loud and an underslept person isn't resilient enough against noise.

The next morning it happened again. This time he opened his eyes before the garbage men came. He kept looking at the ceiling, and his tired mind projected designs from the Saint Petersburg library onto the white surface. Riina had signed him in as a guest at reception so that she could show him around. Ever since she had left, over a year ago, he kept searching the web for airfares, booking them, packing. Or he was waiting for her to write that she was coming. He was always saying hello or goodbye. Sometime during the middle of the week he got an incredible urge to make love with her. He rolled onto her side of the bed, then onto his. Then he realized that there wasn't her side and his, he was sleeping alone in a big bed.

'How are you getting on without a woman?' Çem asked him about once a week. Usually it was on Friday over a drink, or at their regular sweet Mondays. Every Monday someone either baked something or brought a few cakes from a bakery. It was a company tradition. Two years running. 'Watch, everyone will only take one piece!' his Turkish colleague said before the first such event. Then they laughed about their colleagues choking when Mika finished the rest of the cakes. Çem paid him out his bet and invited him for sweet salmiakki, a drink that tasted like melted liquorice candy, and was heavy and sticky like asphalt. 'Now you know the two most abhorrent things in this country: the one-cake-and-done rule and salmiakki.'

Later Çem joked: 'Let him eat, he needs sugar.' He winked at Mika, 'or is it women who replace sex with sugar?' A female colleague said that she would not tolerate such statements, and she went to eat her cake in the kitchenette. Çem knew he had to go apologize. That was another thing he hated about this country—no sexist jokes! It hung in the air on an invisible yellow Post-it note. There were Post-it notes everywhere. In the kitchenette: 'Make sure the electric teakettle is off.' In the bathroom: 'Make sure the door is locked.' As if he wanted nothing more than to urinate with the door open. He and Mika had a good laugh about it. They laughed about the things that the locals didn't notice, and as Çem put it, which subconsciously stressed them, therefore all their colleagues saw a psychologist.

'It's not true that men need it and women can live without it!' Riina said, angry. She called it a stupid sexist stereotype. But that didn't address the fact that Mika missed her. That white body with the circulatory system visibly drawn under the skin. When she was writing her term papers, the visits dropped off. When she came back afterwards, he wasn't able to make love with her. He used to like being able to jump on her at the door, walk in on her in the shower, cuddle her all the time. He said he was accumulating heat. Then all of a sudden he couldn't. 'I'm not a wind-up toy!' he said, irritated. He went to lie down on the sofa, but came back in the middle of the night. He cuddled up to Riina, and as he was falling asleep, he felt pressure between his legs.

'You've turned me into a nutjob who has to get an appointment with a psychologist! A psycho, just like in your thick books, where people spend 200 pages thinking about their mother!' that was the thought that occurred to him as he was staring at the ceiling. He wondered what he'd say to her during her next visit. Maybe he'd just send her an email. 'Like an old man!' he thought. He couldn't stand having anyone in the apartment any more. When Riina would come over, he'd get irritated. She'd use things that she hadn't touched in weeks. She'd walk around in panties with the days of the week on them and an ugly pyjama top, supposedly Russian retro. She'd make herself four cups of coffee a day, and read musty books! She'd talk nonsense. She'd complicate everything. She no longer enjoyed anything the way she used to. He no longer enjoyed anything the way he used to. He couldn't sleep.

After a point, he started to like those morning moments. It was a strange time that disappeared between night and day. He'd think about himself, about her, and then he'd try to put it together and think about them. Riina admitted that she had been offered a spot in the doctoral program in Saint Petersburg, but she was thinking about the States. 'Where could you find out more about the Russian soul than from an old Cold War enemy!' she said, laughing. He didn't laugh. When she got an acceptance letter from a university in some cornfield in the States, he knew there was no *us* any more. His mother gave him a letter organizer. It was her way of giving a green light to their long-distance relationship. He couldn't believe it: life with Riina had transported him to the century of steam. He could see himself sitting behind a writing desk and using the morning moments of neurotic insomnia to write long letters. He'd make trips to the post office. He visited his local Helsinki post office once in a while when he went to pick up his box of Horalky from his mother. That absurd habit his Turkish colleague laughed at. Çem could find Turkish products in the grocery store on the politically-correctly-labelled 'exotic food' shelves, but Mika couldn't find any Slovak specialties in Helsinki grocery stores, and once in a while he craved them. He'd go to the Russian grocery store Kalinka to buy prepared horseradish and pickles. And he'd go to the post office for Horalky.

'This is a very modern relationship! Many people live like this in these globalized times!' Riina protested. Riina enjoyed living between worlds. Either in books or on airplanes. He was stuck between waking and dreaming. He woke up and planned his day. He tried to focus on simple things. 'What do you think about when you can't sleep?' he asked his grand-mother when he spoke to her on the phone. She had had trouble sleeping for years. She told him that she thought about what to make for lunch, mentally picked out her clothes for the next day, and then she thought about what she wore after the war when she went to the ministry office to request paper. How she had to look good and flirt for an order of pencils and lined notebooks. She had a red dress with two rows of buttons and a light summer hat that looked really good on her. At home everyone said 'You're our Gina Lollobrigida!' Her neighbour had a cat named Lollobrigida! It used to do its business on their flowers and dig up the bulbs. She recalled the kinds of flowers her mother planted in the garden and which tree was where. She went one by one, as if she were walking through the garden, once in a while she bent down to pick up an apple and said: this is where the raspberry bushes used to be! So he started to plan too. Instead of putting it in his laptop where he had a clever program that replaced a planner, he wrote everything he had to do in his head. But all of his lists led to Riina.

He used the morning hours he gained to research some phrases on Google. *Rid of her. Je suis venu te dire que je m'en vais. Bye, bye, baby, bye, bye.* Break-up lines from songs. It made him laugh. He hadn't felt so lighthearted for a long time. He decided not to look for any more flights or trek back and forth across the visa border. Riina would be the one to fly back. She'd look forward to it, read, and file images of their lovemaking between the pages. The tremors of transport would be like foreplay. She'd have to concentrate to finish a chapter. She'd fly over, and when she flew back, she'd be holding back tears. Her ears would plug, which is very painful on a plane. The higher the plane would climb, the worse the pain would get.

NATÁLIA, PARIS

A Postcard for the Black Men of Paris

Perhaps under the influence of UNICEF postcards on which Black children with large round heads and flies in the corners of their eyes ask for your help, Natália had a penchant for dragging lonely Black men into an already overcrowded apartment. The front door opened onto the living room where there was a bed under the window opposite a pullout sofa. In the bedroom, three beds were pushed so close together that there was only a narrow passage to the bathroom. The apartment had no closets; Natália hadn't unpacked since her arrival. In the morning she'd just reach under the bed and pull her clothes out of her suitcase. Pierre, a Canadian who took turns with her behind the bar, laughed, saying they lived like the Chinese. Legally the apartment could have four people living in it. The landlady was an Italian woman with a cigarette in the corner of her mouth and a moped helmet under her arm. She always forgot to bring something, dug in the large purse hanging off her elbow, and dropped ashes from her cigarette onto the carpet. The landlady suspected that there weren't four stable tenants living in the apartment. The faces kept changing. Six to ten people slept wherever they could. But as long as they kept paying, and the neighbours didn't complain about noise, everything was fine. The landlady would take the rent in cash, close her purse, and ride her moped to the next apartment.

The apartment was usually quiet. In the morning the curtains were drawn until the women from the night shift got up. Then the day shift women would start to trickle in, as well as the ones who had gone to town looking for work. They cooked, watched TV, cursed their colleagues individually, and the French people collectively. The quietest sex also took place in this apartment. It was so quiet that in the morning Natália thought it didn't happen. She turned to the wall only to find a huge Black man from the Antilles breathing next to her. He was still sweating hormones, which made him smell of fish.

When they came home from an Antillean club, she let him make her a meal out of what she had: tomato, banana, and honey. Her shelf in the fridge was empty. Other times it was chicken and rice. 'And sauce. In Africa you'll never be served meat on its own. It always comes with a sauce,' a guy from Benin said. A guy from Cameroon said he was a prince, and made a simple omelette. When they finished eating, they made love behind the bushes in the park. His butt bounced over her as a loud train passed by. She finally didn't have to be quiet with the noise of 12 train cars. Then he asked her to let him borrow her savings. He said he needed the money for a sick uncle in Cameroon. He also said he was looking forward to marrying her and taking her back to Africa, where monkeys ran around the courtyards the way chickens did in French villages. Natália buttoned up, said goodbye, and walked to the metro. Before she lost signal underground, she sent him a text message: 'Ne m'appelle plus!'

For a few weeks, an Indian guy who was in love with her kept calling. They had met on the street. Natália responded to his greeting, showed him the way to the metro, a good old trick, she ate his curry noodles, did yoga with him in the morning. He started to follow her down the streets to the supermarket, and leaving her incredibly long voicemails. At first he was just asking to see her. Then he asked to do yoga with her. His flyers offering classes fluttered all over the neighbourhood. 'No one called,' he cried into the phone. 'Why don't the French want to do yoga?' He talked about the political situation in Sri Lanka, and kept promising to buy her a ticket to go see his parents while he was in exile. He even came up with refugee stories full of illegal documents . . .

But by then Natália had tossed her SIM card into the Seine. She went all the way to Pont Neuf, where, according to her colleague Pierre, all romantic souls of Paris went to jump to commit suicide. 'You're Pont Neuf material,' he said once when he saw her listening to the same CD over and over again and doing a terrible job pouring beer. 'Businessmen and civil servants jump under the metro at La Défénse. But Slavs are romantics. Anna Karenina wouldn't have jumped onto the tracks in Paris either. You're definitely Pont Neuf material.' The SIM card fell from the bridge into the water. It was Natália's floating UNICEF postcard for the Black men of Paris.

Because I'm Attracted to You

She got off the bus on the route from Trenčín, city of fashion, to Bratislava, transfer station, to Paris, city of fashion. She had failed her university entrance exams. When the professor picked up her drawing of the bust of Cicero, he said that she had turned him into a Black man. She should be able to capture the colour of the subject correctly even with charcoal on paper! Black Cicero put Natália well below the university admission cut off. The agency promised her health insurance and a workshop on looking for work abroad. She packed her high heels, pantyhose, and a few blouses to be able to dress up for interviews. She also put printed resumes in her suitcase. On the agency's recommendation, she invented a few references from Trenčín restaurants. Not too flashy though, so that the employers wouldn't get the idea to call the phone numbers and check on her waitressing skills.

She had never carried a lunch plate further than from the kitchen stove to the Sunday table in the living room. An Egyptian owner of a pizzeria asked her to take an order to table thirteen. Five plates at once. Beverages first! Coffee afterwards, and it should be added to the check under the corner of the tablecloth. She didn't know about the checks, so she brought coffee to her whole section for free. The next day he asked her to greet and seat the guests. Why did she seat the couple into the next section? Was she trying to give them

privacy? During the lunch rush? On the third day she started
bright and early. She was supposed to vacuum, wipe the tables,
and set out the utensils. She was still polishing the water
glasses when the first guests started to arrive. On day four she
was assigned to clean the bathrooms. The owner must have
noticed that she hadn't wiped under the seat with a rag; she
just brushed the bowl and used air freshener. He told her to
wash her hands and go buy meat. She bungled the name of
the store, so people on the street couldn't give her directions.
After wandering the neighbourhood for half an hour, she had
to go back. The meat had already been purchased. Two new
women from Ukraine were serving the pizza, the cleaning was
left up to a Black guy, and an older lady from former
Yugoslavia was cleaning the toilets. A little boy from the street
stopped at the bar. The bartender couldn't even see him. He
asked for a glass of water. Natália went to get it for him. The
owner of the pizzeria took it out of her hand, gave it to the
boy, and said: 'Here you are, but don't get used to getting
water here, OK? I don't want to see you again!' The boy
nodded, drank the water in one breath, and ran off. Natália
didn't get any more text messages with a time to show up.

She put on her pantyhose again, which turned into a
second skin in the 30-degree heat. The first time she had worn
high heels was to her prom, then to graduation. Remembering
those events, she taped both of her heels. She walked to the
nearest metro station and went to a random stop. She told
herself that she'd get off when she felt like it. At the station
exit, a Maghreb-looking man grabbed her elbow. 'Are you lost,
Miss?' When she told him she was looking for work, he said

he was too. 'Let's look together!' He bared his white teeth. The man held her elbow tightly. He matched her step. Whenever she turned to look at him, he gave her a broad smile. As if he were betting everything on that perfect row of white teeth, and it worked. He wrote down her number, and before Natália's heels clicked down the stairs of the next metro station, he had already sent her a message: 'Stop looking! You found me!'

She had been told not to rely on posted flyers and ads. The important thing was knowing how to present yourself. Perhaps they don't even know that they need someone. The agency recommended healthy assertiveness. A smile and a firm handshake. She stopped at a restaurant where the manager sat her down at a table and went to make coffee. 'Come in! You have to speak up! Don't be afraid!' he said at the door. While he was making two espressos, she took a look around. She tried to imagine herself spending a minimum of eight hours a day there for the next few months. She'd get to know every painting on the wall, the utensils and the china, the coffeemaker and the kitchen, the carpet pattern . . . Whenever the restaurant would be empty, like it was now, she'd count the flowers on the replicas of the impressionists from behind the bar. The manager set the coffee in front of her, sat down facing her, and looked at Natália for a long time, then he put on his glasses and carefully looked over her resume. 'You have a beautiful restaurant!' she said. The manager lifted his eyes from the resume and looked at her once more. 'And you're a beautiful woman.' Natália didn't respond, but shivers ran down her sweaty back. Out of learned politeness the corners of her mouth lifted into a smile before she had a chance to consider her reaction. Even the slight smile frightened her. 'I'll give you a job, but it's going to be difficult,' he said after he took off his glasses and set the resume down on the table in front of him. 'It's going to be difficult, because I'm attracted to you.'

She thought about that sentence, sitting across from L'Arc de Triomphe. The statues rippled in the hot air, they were suggesting a decisive step, they gesticulated wildly. The allegorical being in charge of that chaos had its mouth wide open and its shouting replaced the sound of traffic through the roundabout. The restaurant walls were faded, the impressionists had taken on blue hues from the sun, the carpet was worn between the tables. Her upper lip buzzed lightly from the hot espresso. She took pictures of a few tourists under the arch, ate noodles at a Chinese buffet, re-taped her heels in the bathroom, and went on. To hand in her resume at one more place at least, and then she'd go home.

At an Irish pub, the owner took her resume, sat down on a bar stool, and told her to show up the next day to train. 'I bet he gave you the job because you have Irish red hair,' said Pierre, Natália's Canadian colleague from the Irish pub. 'I colour it,' Natália said. 'Don't worry, I won't tell him,' Pierre said jovially. 'Underline for me the things that are true,' he said with a smile as he looked at Natália's resume. 'It's a good thing you chose the right hair colour . . .' 'Your hair looks like you've washed it in the Kilkenny,' a regular said to Natália, looking at her through a glass of reddish Irish beer. 'He lives in an apartment above the establishment, and he has a wife and kids. I don't get how he can flirt with you like that,' Pierre said, but after the man's subsequent visits he just shook his head and smiled. 'Give me your hand,' the regular reached over the bar. 'Come on, I just want to hold your hand. Your hands don't get any rest all day . . .' He covered the palm of her hand with his other hand: 'A sandwich!' he said, 'Pour me another Kilkenny to go with it!'

Despite the hot Paris summer, she looked thin and pale in the mirror across from the bar. 'You want to go out into the world? You don't even know how to cook! You'll be eaten alive!' her mother said to her before she left. For a month she had been making herself couscous with tomatoes and eating white rolls that her roommate Petra brought home from the hotel. Over the bar she looked into the mirror with the etched beer logos. 'Look at yourself!' the regular said. 'Do you know that painting? Go see it at a gallery! We'll go see it together. I'll show it to you!' He said she looked like a lady from a Renoir painting. The lady standing behind a bar, looking out. A bartender with red hair. Natália looked out. She pulled her hair tighter in a hairband. She parted it in the middle. She leaned against the bar. She thought about that painting. For her entrance exams she had studied art history. The regular lifted his glass of red beer and looked through it at Natália: 'Cheers!' he said.

Listen to Everyone, Forget Everything

She was looking at the small window above the beds. Once in a while a blue light flashed by when a fire truck was leaving the station across the street. She was trying not to fall asleep yet. The Irish pub closed at one. Natália could go home at 12:30, because Pierre was always the one to close. He chatted with the guests, towel over his shoulder, amicably leaning over the bar, washing glassware with one hand while smoking with the other. 'Be sympathetic and listen to everyone, but when you leave the establishment, forget everything you heard,' he said. He locked the pub, got on his bike, and disappeared into the darkness. She didn't know where he lived, who he lived with, or what he did when he wasn't pouring beer. She had heard him speak English with a Canadian accent, seen him hit the bullseye with one dart after another, heard him play traditional Irish songs on the fiddle, and watched him kick a bagpiper out of the pub. Pierre said he was playing too loud. 'A bagpipe isn't a musical instrument, it's a weapon! Natália, count the glasses, make sure that none of them cracked!'

In the dark, she listened to the sleeping women breathe, and kept an ear out for Petra coming up the stairs. Then she sat in the bathroom on a closed toilet, and Petra sat on the edge of the bathtub. Natália told her about the clients at the Irish pub. Some of them came every night. Others had their days and habits. There were some who only showed up once, but something about them caught Natália's attention. In the apartment where someone was always sleeping, everything happened quietly. Whenever Petra wanted to laugh, she would open her mouth but she'd have to put a hand over it to suppress the sound. Natália told her about a client who drank from a small glass, but he'd have four or five in a night. That way his beer didn't get warm. He drank slowly, in a cultured manner, as if it were wine. According to Natália, his movements were gay. Or aristocratic. And his name was Louis to boot. Then there was a huge Irishman who came to play darts. His Japanese wife always came with him, drank wine, and Natália admired the jewellery she designed: on Natália's neck, ears, fingers, and blouses. 'You've got a hickey on your neck,' Pierre said to Natália. 'Must be a metal allergy, huh?' The Japanese designer winked at her. 'You should stop wearing that necklace, and it'll get better in a couple of days.' Petra always laughed until someone banged on the bathroom door and they'd have to pipe down.

Natália woke up in the middle of the night because Petra was stirring in the bed next to hers and mumbling something. All of a sudden she sat up, and with her eyes closed she spoke in French: 'The elevator doesn't work, take the bags down the stairs!' The bags were used for dirty linens. Petra didn't say much about working at the hotel. She did her job, and then she took the leftover bread, honey, and jam packets from the hotel breakfast in a clean bag. Every morning there was a black plastic bag with yesterday's bread on the table at the apartment. There was plenty for everyone. Petra was the only White, young, and small-built woman at work. When she came to the reception desk with her resume asking for a job at the hotel, the receptionist leaned over the counter and said: 'Have you ever seen a femme de chambre? The women who clean here are as big as armoires to have the strength to move furniture and clean several floors of rooms a day. Are you up to it?' It didn't scare Petra off. She said she was a swimmer and could use the strength training. She pulled up her sleeve and showed the receptionist her biceps. The receptionist laughed, dialled a number, and said to someone: 'Your new maid is here.'

The first few days Petra slept like a log after work. She even snored a little and talked in her sleep. Then she got used to it and started to go swimming at a pool close to her apartment. Work, pool, cooking for two to three days ahead, sleep. 'Maybe I should also start swimming,' Natália said. Her heart pounded for at least an hour after work from the people and the smoke. Then she fell asleep and woke up in a daze around noon, the curtains drawn at all times. She wandered around the apartment, turned the TV on without sound, flipped through the paper that someone kept bringing from the metro. Her phone rang, and the Cameroonian prince wanted to meet her at a park. On the way to the park her phone rang again, and she promised to have dinner with the Indian guy. During dinner a text message came in, the Algerian who had photos of his kids in his wallet wanted to see her. But she had already promised to go dancing with the Antillean cook.

She sat in the park on a spread-out map of Paris, listened to the guy from Benin sing, and accompanied him on a small drum. At a table in a Turkish coffee shop, she watched the animated Algerian. He told her he'd call her every day when he went to spend the summer with his family in Algeria. Natália was standing over a metro grate when the first car pushed up warm air. The Antillean cook held her and whispered something about her butt and breasts. Natália either didn't hear or didn't understand. The metro roared past, and the gust of warm air dissipated into the night. 'You should improve your French,' he said.

'You have to speak perfect French here.' She was serving herself halušky with a plastic spoon at a Slovak picnic. 'You have to master French. Better than the French themselves,' Helena said, laughing. Natália handed her the pot, and Helena ate some halušky. Tiny, very thin, strictly elegant, with jewellery from the Japanese designer. A theatre actress. She could play a French woman any day and get a standing ovation. Petra met her at the pool. They started out speaking French before they figured out where they were both from. Helena had brought a pot of halušky to the picnic at the park. After three years in the city, she became a French woman of Slovak origin. More French than the French. Petra was about halfway there. Soon she was going to stop working at the hotel. Become a swim instructor. Move to a dorm. Natália tried to draw Petra's portrait. 'I look like I came from a tanning salon,' Petra said, laughing. The portrait remained unfinished under the suitcase.

Their last night together they bought a bottle of good wine and plastic wine glasses on a stem, and set them on napkins with the logo of the hotel Petra had just bid adieu. The plastic clink made them laugh. There was a knock on the door.

Natália was laughing so hard that she inhaled her wine. It came out of her nostrils, like a nosebleed. Tears welled up in her eyes. Petra hugged her and held her tight: 'Call me whenever you need, OK?' she said.

With the Antillean cook she could travel for free. Until he got caught again, he had a prepaid ride on the train from Paris to the suburbs. He leaned against the side of the turnstiles, and jumped over with ease. Natália wanted to do the same, but she couldn't get her legs over the turnstiles. She climbed over and followed the Antillean into the train. She kept looking around nervously, checking for uniformed ticket inspectors with German shepherds on a leash. The Antillean sprawled out comfortably on a seat and picked at the dirt under his nails. She sat down next to him. The stifling air in the tunnel made her tired. She leaned her head on the cook's shoulder and he embraced her. He wanted to kiss her, but she pulled away. Then she remembered that no one knew her in Paris, and she kissed him.

He was taking her to a neighbourhood chez les miens, to his people. Groups of young men stood around between the apartment buildings and spoke verlan, a version of French backwards. He knocked, the door opened, the Antillean walked in and greeted his people. She thought they were going to his place. Instead it was an apartment of some relatives of his. They were watching a soap opera with Black actors, talking, smoking, some were leaving the apartment, others were coming. She sat down on the couch. The family paid no attention to her. The Antillean cook alternately watched what was going on in the living room and on TV and then again the people who were sitting and walking around. The door opened, and a guy sat down on the couch who had café-au-lait-coloured skin, eyes as translucent as a husky's, hair crinkled like crêpe paper, a blond strand here and there, and a wide, freckled nose. Someone hugged him and someone else shook his hand. He set his cell phone on a glass end table, lit a cigarette, and his gaze went back and forth between the soap opera and the living room. She reached out and touched his hair out of curiosity. It wasn't dry or rough like African hair, something was different about its structure, crystals had broken apart and created new bonds. 'Hey, what are you doing??' the guy yelled and threw his unfinished cigarette into the ashtray. Natália started and quickly slipped her hand between her thigh and the couch. 'I asked you what you were doing?? Do I go around touching your hair? Is anyone here touching your hair?' the guy shouted and kept looking at her with his translucent eyes. It occurred to her that he could be wearing contacts, but no, they were his eyes and it was his hair, he was a real mix, quite unusual, and now quite angry. 'Hey, cousin, calm down! Did she hurt you? No!' the cook said and kept watching TV. Natália had noticed that the Antillean called other guys on the street *cousin*, even when all he wanted to do was ask the time. 'Hey, cousin, you got a watch?' And so, in her defence, she told the biracial guy: 'Sorry, cousin!' The guy scoffed, picked up his cell phone from the end table, left the room, and slammed the door. Someone laughed and kept repeating: 'Cousin, cousin!'

Two young women were cleaning a fish in the kitchen and there was rice cooking in a large pot. The cook introduced them to Natália as his cousins. She wanted to help, but she didn't know how to gut a fish. When she lifted the pot lid to stir the rice, she was told that rice doesn't need stirring, the pot only gets shaken. 'I don't know how to cook,' she said to the cousins with a smile. They exchanged a look and then asked her to take plates and utensils to the table. 'Do you know how to set the table?' one of them asked, but the other immediately shushed her and they both laughed. Natália watched how they got their hands dirty with fish blood, how they skilfully gutted the fish with a knife, tossing pieces of skin and bones into a dishpan and the clean meat into a pot. Both had long nails with red nailpolish. She would have loved to sit, like the cook. He sat down in the corner and watched the young women. He was eating yogurt with a spoon. In his big hands, the teaspoon turned into something smaller than a coffee spoon. He kept eating and looking ahead, no one bothered him. Natália just wanted to sit and watch. Take notes, draw sketches. 'Do you want to take those plates?' one of the cousins asked. She knew that 'want' indicated a gentle command in French.

Once in a while she went to African cafeterias. She looked at the large pots, the corpulent women, the mounds of food, the sandals worn helter-skelter, the brightly coloured fabrics. The guy from Benin had taken her to one such cafeteria. They got their food and sat down on a bench at a long table. She went back a few times by herself, but she felt quite uncomfortable. Everyone kept looking at her. She and the Benin guy made a strange couple, but by herself she stuck out like a sore thumb.

The Cameroonian prince sat her down at a table in his family's house. His sister was cooking. She wore a simple dress, like most African women Natália had seen in Paris. Two strips of cloth with an opening for the head in the middle, very loose, the opening so wide that the dress kept slipping halfway down the women's arms and revealing their shoulders. On her head was a turban from loosely wound cloth. Natália wanted to know how the cloth was tied, but she was afraid to ask. The sister sat at the table, all serious, on her right sat her husband, an old, sick, White man. The food smelt good, the sister served and asked questions. She wanted to know how many siblings Natália had. When she said that she was an only child, the sister laughed. 'In Africa we can have 10 or more siblings.' The sister surmised that the country Natália was from had a similar law to China's, limiting the number of children. Natália looked to the sister's husband for support. But he only stared into his plate. He didn't say anything the whole time, except thanking her for the food and he shuffled off to his room. The people at the table were the husband, the sister, the supposed Cameroonian prince, and Natália. The prince and his sister looked healthy and strong. The sister was stocky, he was brawny, with naturally outlined muscles. The sister's husband was leaning over the plate, his fingers looked twisted, he could barely hold a spoon. It was his house. A house with antique French furniture, filled with the aroma of chicken with sauce and rice. Natália wondered whether the man was of sound body and mind. He picked up a glass in his spotted hand and drank some wine. The prince brought him the rest of the bottle to his room. Then he wanted to make love to Natália in the next room, saying that his sister's husband was hard of hearing.

The Antillean cook took Natália to yet another apartment. Once more she thought they were going to his people, that is, to his closest relatives. The Antillean addressed the guy who opened the door as cousin. They talked for a long time, played computer games, and drank coffee. She sat on the balcony and looked at the scorched backyard. Then the Antillean called her into a room and started to undress her. He had borrowed a rubber and the room from the cousin. From the bed Natália kept watching the glass door, behind which the cousin's silhouette kept appearing as he walked around the apartment. She didn't make a peep, and kept shifting around the bed quietly to always keep an eye on the door. When they finished, he tied up the rubber, put on his boxers, and brought a yogurt from the fridge and a small spoon. Natália picked up a clean sheet of paper from the table and found a short Ikea pencil in her bag. As the Antillean sat there, she started to draw him. She captured the main features, that was enough. He had to go. He never said where, and Natália didn't care. She'd go somewhere too. Anywhere. Maybe to an Internet café.

At the café she printed the pictures of plaster busts that get drawn in every class and at every entrance exam. She set the toner to max and the brightness of the paper to minimum. The printer spat out a black Napoleon, a black Cicero, a black *renaissance boy*, and a black *bust of an old man . . .*

Batat, Yam, and Other Kitsch

On the clearance shelf at a bookstore she found a paperback by René Depestre. Its cover caught her eye: it had a stylized dark-skinned woman with vines twisting around her. It wasn't clear which was completing the other—the vines the woman, or the woman the vines. The title of the book was *Woman— Garden*. Natália was on her way to the Irish pub, but she had left early enough to be able to walk around town. She had the time to turn the book over and read about the author. She set it down, then she picked it back up and flipped through the first few pages. The price was covered with a bright-yellow discount sticker. She walked out of the store clutching a new paperback.

Sometimes she found a CD on clearance. A scratched-up case with a faded photograph. A CD with Antillean music, from the ethnic music series. The cover had a boy with a small drum, and miles of white beaches in the background with thin palm tree trunks. She had also found Jamaica Kincaid, a Caribbean author. The cover of her bestseller had one of Gaugin's Tahitian women. Another colourful cover, bright colours, sun and shadow, fruit, fabrics . . .

Her phone rang; the Antillean cook wanted to see her. Unlike other men, he wasn't high pressure. On the contrary, he was always terribly late. When she saw him approaching with his leisurely stride, she got mad: 'I've been standing in front of this brothel for half an hour!' 'Why didn't you cross the street?' he said and leaned over to kiss her. Natália pulled away and tried again: 'Everyone walking out of here looked at me!' His eyes narrowed, a ripple of a smile crossed his lips: 'Did you enjoy it?' She smiled and kissed him.

He took her to places that weren't exceptional in any way. He avoided downtown, choosing parks, cheap coffee shops, and his relatives' apartments instead. He said little about himself and some of it was made up, as Natália was starting to suspect. She mentioned that she had taken the entrance exam for art school, but hadn't made the cut. She wanted to try again. In response, he said that he was going to try for med school in the autumn. He didn't show the slightest interest in knowing the truth about her. He could see all the relevant things for himself: grey eyes, red hair, white skin, and an accent that he graciously called 'Eastern European'. He had no idea where Trenčín could be . . . or Slovakia for that matter. He said the name of the country as if it were some fruit that was difficult to describe. Like a batat, a yam, or a topinambur. *Slovaquie.*

He didn't pry, didn't ask any questions, he just moved around town, said *uh-huh*, and looked at himself in every reflective surface. 'Stop looking at yourself!' Natália would sometime say, laughing. Instead, he'd stop in the middle of the pavement, sway slowly, ball up, grab his head and his balls while dancing, step in place in his worn-out shoes. He was dancing with his own reflection in a store window. Natália laughed and pushed him off the pavement. He didn't say a word, didn't explain anything, never got offended. Sometimes he disappeared, other times he showed up. He'd ring the door-bell downstairs and want to come up. If he didn't show up for some time, he'd mumble something, but he'd never apologize. He never had money, but he didn't complain. He always showed up late, but said that nothing had held him up. He didn't say much about the Antilles either. Only that it's hot and beautiful there. Anyone who hadn't been there could have said as much. He spoke in short sentences that had no future or past tense. Only about common occurrences anyone could have observed. 'You have such beautiful eyes! I've never noticed.'

Once again she sat him down to draw his portrait. The dry grass in the park was prickly; ants were crawling on the tree bark. There was no shop in sight where they could buy water or have a cup of coffee. It was a park somewhere in the suburbs; she had no idea why he had taken her there. They must have seen all the suburban parks by now. She sat leaning against a tree. He was sitting in the grass across from her, unable to sit still in a pose, always fidgeting, giggling, com-menting about the heat, shaking his shirt with a fiery dragon on it, throwing grass he had torn up at Natália. She started to draw him, a still mask, but he turned, so she captured his face from a different angle, but then he was looking into the sun, squinting, so she redrew the head from below . . . Then it was his turn. He turned over the page, took a good look, put the pencil in his mouth, measured, and kept leaning his head from side to side. In the end he drew a lopsided circle for the head, dots for the eyes, and a line for the mouth. But his imitation of Natália drawing was spot on.

For a few days she had heavy cramps in her lower abdomen. A pregnancy test came back negative. So did a second one. Petra told her to buy a third and not believe it. Natália started to scribble a face of a biracial child. Maybe the child would look like the 'cousin' whose hair she had touched. She followed the signs at the hospital, and sat down in the gynaecology department waiting area. The doctor gave her a stern look. He tried to identify her accent. Lying on the table, she kept looking through the blinds, wondering whether the doctor always left them open in plain view of the hospital courtyard, or if it was simply that he hadn't bothered to close them for her.

Not long after, she got a phone call to come back. She had to start spending the savings from the bottom of her suitcase to cover the cost of the appointments and prescriptions. Waiting outside of doctors' offices took up all of her free time. If she had any left, she wandered aimlessly around the neighbourhood. Sometimes she sat by the canal in the 10th arrondissement. She went outside to cry. Everyone in the apartment was supposed to think that she just had the flu. She poured water over her couscous and chopped a tomato. No longer with honey and a banana. 'I'm clean. Just yesterday my cousin and I went to get tested,' the Antillean said on the phone. The antibiotics worked quickly, but she kept going to the canal. She would sit down on the warm stones, read paperbacks, call Petra from her new SIM card, and then she'd draw picnickers and objects floating on the water until sunset.

Are You Afraid, My Love?

She went back to a spot where she had once waited for the Antillean. She pulled aside the blue velvet curtain with cigarette holes in it. Of course, she didn't want to lounge around the armchairs with the blonde Polish girls. She was going to try to get a job as the coat-check girl. The manager made her coffee, looked her up and down, and asked her if she wouldn't like to be a hostess. She'd make more money. The coat-check position had already been filled, he just forgot to take down the sign.

While the owner of the establishment was making coffee, Natália took a look around. Two blondes were slumped on their tail bones, buried in soft armchairs impregnated with bar stench. The smell was very familiar. Pierre closed the pub, she opened it. She always came in early to unlock. As she opened the door, mustiness would waft out. Smoke absorbed into the wallpaper and the wood. Dried beer stains. She was constantly washing those off the bar. Beer was sticky and smelt bad. Rings after liqueurs, wine, and juices. Elbows leaning on the counter would stick, and when they got unstuck, a few hairs would remain on the bar. She quickly lit a cigarette to cover over the stench with smoke. Then she set the chairs down, turned down the keg chillers, and poured out the first glass from each tap. She turned on the cash register and opened the door. The first customer was the regular from upstairs. He sat down in the empty pub and asked for a reddish Kilkenny on tap. One more. Oh, just one more. Then other guests arrived.

For example, a Slovak woman with glasses. She came in and read in the corner. She was there almost daily before her study trip was done. She always came alone, had a coffee and a large Guinness, and talked about her American love. A few nights she stood leaning on the corner of the bar, waiting for Natália to have a free moment. While Natália cleared glasses or wiped the bar, the other woman talked. About her love, who had an apartment with a terrace in Sarajevo and a job she loved. More about her. One time a tall young woman came into the bar. She had an odd haircut, as if someone had cut her hair with dull scissors. Her bag still had airport tags. She came up to the woman with glasses and hugged her from behind as the former was talking about the latter. Natália poured another Guinness and went to pick up glasses around the pub. She turned up her favourite CD and the second round was on her. 'We love seeing happy endings taking place in our bar,' Pierre said as they were changing shifts.

And then there was the guy who came in early one evening, when the only other person at the bar was the regular from the upstairs apartment. He told Natália what music to put on. He showed her his tattoos. He said she looked like his sister. He promised to have her name tattooed somewhere, and told her to pick a spot. He offered places that would hurt, where there was bone, even his forehead. 'Here?' he asked one night. He showed the gum line above his upper teeth. He said it was the only spot where a tattoo would be preserved if his body burned. He was a fireman. He only drank one small beer, and even that took him forever. He kept telling her how long it took him to climb up a ladder to the fifth floor. He talked about cutting victims out of car wrecks and the extra pay for carrying corpses out of burning buildings. People kept turning away and looking into their glasses. The Japanese jewellery designer felt faint and went outside to light her Slim. He also talked about beautiful things. About dancing angels. How it was the last thing a person saw in a room full of flames when all the air was gone. The future victim would squat on the ground, and if he looked up, spinning blue flames would flash right under the ceiling. No one had ever seen anything more beautiful. Then there would be an explosion. The fireman boasted that he had never needed to go see a psychologist. He just had his small beer at the Irish pub.

One more! A secret poet, the phantom of Paris. He printed small books of poems. He also illustrated them, bound them, and cut them. Then he put them in frequented places. On park benches, on metro seats, he placed them in store catalogues, set them under glasses like coasters.

Natália looked at one of the Polish women. A hostess in a worn out armchair. She had eczema on her arms and legs, and a blister on her lip. She would soon be fired. The sign on the door was a search for her replacement. When the owner offered Natália to be a hostess, she realized there was no coat-check position. She waited for the coffee to cool down a little, drank it, and left. She wanted to take back her resume, but then it occurred to her that the Polish woman may want to call her. On a whim. She'd take her to the African cafeteria to eat chicken and rice. Or she'd try to cook something for her.

Maybe she'd try to gut a fish. And she'd make a salad out of tomatoes and bananas, with herbs, oil, and honey. The UV light at the brothel made the eczema stand out. Like all white things: teeth, the whites of the eyes, tennis shoes.

Natália walked home from work at night. Her heart beat as loudly as her heels. When she closed the door of the apartment, the beating gradually settled down. She opened the curtain on the French window. 'How that moon shines, the dead and the living ride a horse, are you afraid, my love?' Her grandfather would always say that during a full moon. The phosphorescent face of the moon looked like it had eczema on its cheeks. Out of the window she could see the fire station across the street. A car flew by in the blue light, noise at the end of the street died down. Only the voices of Paris regulars could be heard.

Love and Travel

It was a strange sight. Natália came home from work late at night. Her boyfriend was sitting at the table with a plastic tablecloth and crumbs from breakfast. Her roommates were sitting around on their beds, even though usually everyone would have already been asleep at that hour. They sat and waited. When Natália opened the door, some of them stood up and started to move around the apartment. They pretended to get a glass of water in the kitchen, check how the laundry was drying on the rack, or look out the window. Natália's boyfriend sat at the table, and the sight of him made her laugh. 'I came to get you,' he said.

Igor had driven for two days, he got the address from Natália's parents, and now he was there. Natália's occasional text messages didn't look right to him. She never called, she only answered his calls. If she actually heard her phone at the pub. Her roommates kept watching him. Some were simply concerned that another person would squeeze into the apartment for a few weeks. He had thrown his sleeping mat under the table, but he left his backpack in the car. Others' gazes were saying something else.

Back when they had said goodbye at the train station in Trenčín, when he was printing Natália's resumes at his father's office, they were so close! Now she just went into the kitchen and brought herself some old bread and packets of butter and honey. She asked him if he was hungry, and then she started to eat her dinner. Igor wondered whether he had ever felt more embarrassed. The last time must have been in elementary school, when his mother made him get up in front of the whole class and tell them that he had lice. He thought about sleeping in his car. He looked over the roommates once more, wondering which one of them Natália was dating. He decided to stay quiet and wait. Maybe one of them would speak. He was even ready for a slap. But the apartment was silent, the curtains were drawn, the TV was on mute. The only sound was the chewing of a baguette.

'Let's go for a walk,' Natália said when she finished eating. They walked out onto the nighttime street and went to the nearest park. Igor started to talk about his parents, about himself, and about the friends they had in common. How everyone was doing. Natália paused over the metro grate and waited for the rush of warm air. 'I wanted to show you something, but I can't right now,' she said. 'Are you seeing someone?' Igor asked. 'Have you lost it? I wanted to show you hot air blowing out of here when the metro goes by, but the next one won't come until morning.' Igor continued: 'Do you want to be a waitress, live in an apartment with . . . how many of you are there? Don't you want to take another shot at the entrance exams?' He also said that their kitchen window looked onto a sewer, that firemen looked into their windows all day and made lewd gestures, that the only thing her roommates were interested in was who made how much money and who put what in the fridge and where. It made Natália laugh. Igor had been sitting at the table since noon, he had met everyone, and talked to all of them. He had plenty of time to evaluate her situation. They were sitting on the park bench where the Antillean cook had put his hand under Natália's panties and said: 'I'll just warm my hand.' He ended up in her bed at the apartment and in the morning he smelt like fish.

'Should we go home?' she asked. Igor took her hand and led her through the park back to the apartment. In the morning he helped her pack while she worked out with her roommate that she was leaving without notice: 'What a bitch you are! You didn't tell us you had a boyfriend, or that you were leaving.' Natália promised to put up an ad at the internet cafe and pay the rent for the remaining two weeks of the month. A 100 euro so that her roommate wouldn't say that a man with a fishy smell had slept there. 'Yuck, he stank!' the roommate had said in the morning, after he left. She also wouldn't say that Natália often spent the night away from the apartment. She put the money in a can and locked it in her suitcase. 'What will you tell them at work?' she asked. Natália didn't say anything. She just didn't show up, and Pierre had to work the shift alone. Then he put an ad on the door. He called Natália, but by then another SIM card was floating on the Seine.

In the meantime, Natália was taking pictures with Igor in front of L'Arc de Triomphe. He treated her to a coffee and a croissant on the Champs-Élysées. They marvelled at the view from the Sacré Coeur: 'I can't believe you never came here!' They had lunch on the terrace of a restaurant that served oysters, frogs, and escargot, among other things. Igor rubbed blisters on his feet and couldn't walk any more. He drove barefoot all the way to Trenčín. She looked at his left hand on the steering wheel. Then she put his right hand in her lap and said: 'I'll warm your hand.' They made love in a parking lot in Germany.

The next summer she got out to pee in the same parking lot. Then she got back on the bus. Through dirty glass she watched the flat, well-manicured countryside go by. She got a job as a waitress in Berlin. She lived in one of the hotel rooms above the restaurant. An Italian synthesizer duo lived in the next room. The owner had given them a job for the summer playing on the terrace for the guests as they ate their seafood specialties. When one of them would get really drunk, he'd bang on Natália's door: 'Bella, amore, caro!' She'd crawl over the balcony to a colleague's room and sleep on her couch.

JULIANA, BUDAPEST

Local Lore

In Budapest, the buses still use the old ticket punches. Only people from the former Eastern bloc know how to use them. Insert and pull. The machine punches holes in the ticket in a specific number combination. Juliana could easily identify foreigners on a bus, because they'd insert the ticket and wait. Then they'd pull it out and look for the punched-out code. The locals would sit on the leatherette seats that had yellow foam sticking out of them and look on. Ticket inspectors were rare in above-ground transportation. Most of them were on the metro, and mostly on the blue line.

At the end of the blue line, one had to transfer from an ancient Russian-made metro train to a Hungarian-made Ikarus bus. Juliana remembered those buses from Bratislava. The red-and-white railings in Budapest also looked the same as they did in Slovak cities. As did the details of the buildings, the furniture, and the clothes. She could get by with Slovak to buy her fruits and vegetables: narancs, paradiscom, krumpli. People's faces reminded her of her friends in Bratislava. The university near St. Stephen's Basilica, where Juliana was studying, offered a Western-style education. In one corner of the square was the California Coffee Company—WiFi and muffins, and right next to it were souvenir shops and restaurants serving halászlé and goulash. The boards outside advertised the goulash to tourists.

Juliana came to the white-night discotheque in blue jeans and a red hoodie. She and two of her classmates wandered in, unaware that the dress code for the night was anything white. Juliana, the American Jackie, and the Romanian Cristina. Cristina's boyfriend wasn't allowed in. Those were the rules of the night: anything white and no men. They were among the first at the establishment. The area around the bar was filling up very slowly. They walked up and down, sipped beer from their mugs, tried playing pool. The dance floor was empty. They could hardly imagine anyone plucking up enough courage to dance that night. Or to pick up the microphone and sing karaoke. At midnight, the glassware ran out and the bar shifted to plastic. White tank tops gleamed on the dance floor under the UV lights. There was a line for the microphone in front of the screen that played videos with lyrics.

A tall woman with the most beautiful arms at the party put her arm around Juliana's shoulders. At least that was Juliana's impression of her. She breathed the local beer Dreher at her and dragged her off to dance to a popular song. She was wearing thin bracelets, necklaces, and belly chains. The only reason her English was good even in her drunken state was that she was from London. She had come to Budapest for a fencing tournament. That explained the arms. 'Why aren't you wearing white?' she shouted into Juliana's ear. She had to leave early in the morning. For her flight back to London. She wrote her number on Juliana's hand. Juliana wrote hers on that exquisite arm.

In the morning, the English woman got stopped by ticket inspectors at the entrance to the blue line. She had to go back to the ticket window. There was a note on the window, but the only thing she understood was the number 15. There was no one inside, only a knitted sweater tossed over a chair and a pack of cigarettes on the table. A line snaked in front of the window, the tourists shifted nervously from foot to foot, taking off their heavy backpacks. After the metro she transferred to a bus that took her to the airport. She battled the ticket punch the whole way. No one helped her, no one spoke to her. People kept looking ahead, some even looked right at her. It occurred to her that the locals' faces weren't white, but grey.

She set off the metal detector. An airport employee checked her with rehearsed movements. She asked her to take off her jewellery. Her hand luggage passed under the rubber strips into the X-ray machine. She checked that her cell phone was off. She took a window seat. As the plane took off, the pressure forced her to keep swallowing. Her mouth was dry and her throat was sore from the cigarette smoke. She regretted having drunk the local beer from plastic cups. Next time, she'd only drink an import, Becks in a glass bottle. The beer was making her burp. As soon as the seatbelt light went off, she went to the bathroom. She washed her face. In the mirror she noticed a number written on her arm. Her pupils were dilated from exhaustion, the whites of her eyes were red from smoke. She recalled having danced with someone. Too bad she hadn't had more time. For the famous goulash. For a spa. She washed off the scribbles from her arm and returned to her seat.

She flipped through the onboard magazine that recommended spicy Hungarian cuisine and authentic Turkish baths. Reading made her feel nauseous, so she put the magazine back into the seat pocket in front of her and checked that there was an air-sickness bag. She didn't like the city. Grass growing over the curbs, peeling stucco, broken park benches, bumpy trams. Women with plastic shopping bags. The old ones looked tired, the young ones wore too much makeup. She opened her triangle sandwiches and asked the flight attendant for a blanket. She didn't mind the air conditioning. She just wanted to get some sleep; her head was starting to hurt from the beer. She tried to recall whether she had kissed anyone at the establishment. She should probably get a checkup when she got home.

It was already cold in London, but the buses still had the A/C on. She didn't mind, she was used to it. Foreigners sat on the upper deck wrapped in their coats, shivering. She bought a ticket from the driver and took a seat on the lower deck. She watched the pleasant brick facades, the flood of geraniums, a colourful crowd on Oxford Street. She had read that the Budapest parliament building was based on the one in London. In fact, the one in Budapest was bigger. But it was only fixed up from the Danube side—she remembered the view from the ride on the amphibious bus. The tourists squealed with delight as the bus got in the water, the engine sound changed, the vehicle started to sway differently, and they floated up to the whitish replica of the parliament. The back of the building was grey and blocked off by barricades because of upcoming demonstrations.

Camembert and Good Old Times

Jean-Jacques had two ways to shop. During the week, he went into the 24-hour store under his house and either pulled a pizza out of a freezer or put some hot dogs in his shopping basket. Anything that would be done in a few minutes in the oven or on the stove. By the time his laptop played the Welcome to Windows sound, the food was ready. He put on a movie on his computer, sat down in the shared living room, and after the opening credits he was done with dinner. Then he smoked until the end credits.

Juliana moved in with him shortly after she arrived in Budapest. He wanted to lower his housing expenses; she didn't want to live in a dorm on the outskirts of town. He posted ads in places where foreigners liked to hang out. 'I don't want to live with locals,' he said with no regard for political correctness. Juliana wondered why he didn't live with his girlfriend. From time to time, a Hungarian woman spent the night at their apartment: 'It's good to date the locals for the language and the realia,' Jean-Jacques said without excessive romanticism. He described Emőke with even fewer words: 'Très jolie'. Very pretty.

On Fridays, Jean-Jacques shopped with several of his French colleagues from IBM. Those were different kinds of shopping trips. Shopping trips that took these men back to their roots. At the cheese refrigerator, Jean-Jacques would pick up a cheese labelled Camembert. He'd show it to his colleagues: 'Look, this is camembert!' he'd say and everyone would laugh. Jean-Jacques' father had warned him about the utter disregard for brands in this region. He said he discovered it when he stopped by Tesco following a short visit to the Bratislava French Institute, and one of the bottles claimed to be champagne. He pulled out his glasses, put them on, and read aloud: 'Schampanske!' Then he turned to the woman from the Institute who was accompanying him: 'This isn't shampanske, this is Hubert!' He took off his glasses, but it wasn't until he burst into a hearty laugh that the woman knew she could also start laughing. Then he made her laugh again by the wine shelf. He knelt on the white linoleum scuffed by the black wheels of the shopping carts: 'Devant un bon vin, il faut se mettre aux génoux!' He was kneeling by a bottle with a French label. They set the wine into the shopping cart, and when it ran out, the woman from the Institute was too embarrassed to open anything she had at home and offer it to her guest. She was a fan of wines from the Malé Karpaty region, where her family had a summerhouse on the vineyard slopes. All of a sudden she was sitting on the couch in her own apartment, and nothing in her pantry or in her fridge was good enough for her guest. So she opted for kissing him instead. A long French kiss followed.

Jean-Jacques and his colleagues wandered around the supermarket with their ties loosened, as stiff as boards, cutting off space with their big gestures. They were getting ready for a Friday evening house party followed by a night on the town. Each of them had a multitude of comments, suggestions, and objections about the selection of groceries. Juliana hated it when Jean-Jacques gave her cooking advice while he waited for his hot dogs or pizza. She also hated that he had the poster of a smiling Nicolas Sarkozy in the bathroom, and listened to the sighing CDs of Carla Bruni. But what she hated most was when he'd say 'It's like old times!' referring to Budapest.

'You know what I like about Budapest? It's not the fact that the young women, and sadly, the older ones too, go around dressed as if they had come off the pages of a porn magazine. It's not even the fact that most of them are hookers . . . It's that it's like old times here!' Jean-Jacques liked Budapest, where there were only White people on the metro. 'Just like Paris when my father was young.' Out and about, on public transportation, in cafés, everyone everywhere was White. He went through the Museum of Terror, where two regimes had left black and white faces of their victims, top to bottom. In the middle of the entrance there was a tank with black oil running down it. 'There was one good thing about communism. You know what it was? It protected half of Europe from immigrants. But that won't last . . .' Jean-Jacques' grandfather had fought in Indochina, he had eaten brains directly out of the cracked skull of a living monkey, and he stood so straight on all the photos that the buttons of his uniform could have popped off at any moment. Jean-Jacques' father owned a factory. He walked around as straight as a factory chimney and smoked a cigar. In Budapest, Jean-Jacques got a glimpse of their world.

He didn't want to hang out with the locals. When they spoke, when he saw what and how they ate, how they moved, the illusion fell apart, and these people were nothing more than a weak imitation of old Frenchmen. Juliana never found out what Emőke did for a living. She never stayed long enough for Juliana to have a chance to speak to her. Jean-Jacques didn't eat breakfast. He had a coffee and a cigarette, and went to work. Outside, Emőke took off in a different direction. 'Szíja!' Jean-Jacques would wave to her. He never learnt Hungarian.

The apartment she was sharing with Jean-Jacques had very high ceilings, decorative stucco, and ancient gas heating. Jean-Jacques scrimped so much on heating in the winter, that by the time he came home from work, Juliana was turning book pages in gloves and drinking urinary support tea as a preventative. He talked to her about politics, both French and Hungarian. He introduced her to his colleagues, and told them what she was studying. 'This is my roommate Juliana from Slovakia. Tchéquoslovaquie, he sometimes added for clarification. She's studying philosophy. In English,' he said in a full sentence. Meanwhile, Emőke was sitting on his lap. There was no need to introduce her. If she weren't the one sitting there, someone else would. 'If you want to address a Hungarian girl, chances are that she will have one of three names. They have strange names, but they're all the same.' Jean-Jacques laughed at his observation. All of a sudden Juliana realized why the idiot waiter had ignored her when she was surrounded by foreigners and yelled 'Large Pilsner, please!' three times. Jean-Jacques also drank only Pilsner or French wine.

One morning she found Emőke sitting in the kitchen, smoking. Makeup was streaming down her cheeks. Juliana was surprised that she hadn't taken it off for the night. 'Hogy vagy?' she asked, but she was glad when Emőke wasn't too talkative, because she wouldn't have understood her reply anyway. She had no time for Hungarian alongside her studies. Water was running in the bathroom. Jean-Jacques was shaving. Cold air wafted from the turned off heating. Emőke was sitting there in lacy underwear and his shirt, warming herself with another mint slim. The door slammed and Jean-Jacques left without her. Emőke got up and asked something. Juliana grasped that she wanted to make herself coffee. Kávé. Emőke let the ground coffee boil in the water, the kitchen smelt great. Juliana made herself instant coffee in the morning, which smelt burnt. She inhaled the smell of the coffee and showed Emőke thumbs up. Without a word, Emőke reached for another cup and poured her some.

They sat in silence while Juliana tried to figure out how to tell Emőke that Jean-Jacques was getting on her nerves too. The bathroom door was visible from the kitchen. She opened it and ripped off the smiling Sarkozy. Emőke watched her. In order to make the message clearer, Juliana tore the poster into tiny pieces, threw them into the toilet, and flushed. Emőke started to laugh. She walked over to the fridge, pulled out the real camembert from Friday's shopping trip, opened the dustbin, and threw it in. Then she pulled out another round thing that Jean-Jacques had put on the cheese shelf. Juliana watched in surprise as a Fidorka wafer flew into the dustbin. She had brought it and other sweets for Jean-Jacques. He didn't ask her what it was, and he left it to ripen with similarly shaped cheeses. Now she was laughing about it with Emőke. The Fidorka ended up in the dustbin before Jean-Jacques could open it and find out what an inexplicably disgusting camembert was made in Slovakia.

Awesome, Beautiful

She set the frosty glass on a wobbly bar table. Then she stepped over the chairs piled over with jackets, and tried to catch where the conversation had shifted while she went to get a beer. 'When I lay down, she started to caress me. I really didn't know what to do. So I got up, went to the balcony, and smoked a whole pack of cigarettes. I didn't go back until she was asleep.' She wanted to know who Cristina was talking about. 'Jackie. When she slept at my place after the White party,' Cristina said. 'You're saying that Jackie wanted to sleep with you?' Juliana asked point blank. At the end of the semester Jackie had gone back to the States, to the American South, to her husband.

'I took these pictures when I was 16; magnolias were in bloom in my parents' garden, I had just cut my hair, and I was taking the whole thing all too seriously,' Jackie said, pointing at enlarged photographs of a girl with a strange haircut. She was using the camera's delay timer. 'She looks very shy, and at the same time very sexy,' said Juliana. 'That's exactly how I felt back then.' Jackie kept flipping through her art-work portfolio, as she called it. She finished art school and wanted to go see Europe. School left her with a portfolio of art works and debt. The only way to get to Europe low key, that is, on the cheap, was to go study at a university that offered a scholarship. She couldn't remember why she had chosen

Budapest. In her fridge there was a half-eaten can of sardines and an apple. Nothing else. She offered some to Juliana. She put the sardines on a plate, split the apple in half, and made napkins out of toilet paper. Then she put on some bizarre folk music. As they sat down at the table, Jackie jumped up and took a picture of the sardines on a plate: 'Awesome, beautiful!' she said, laughing.

Before Christmas, Jackie sent her a package of her art— photos of Budapest apartments. The old-school furniture, high ceilings and exterior hallways, gas boilers, tile stoves and the wooden frames of oversized windows and doors, old chandeliers and carpets . . . 'I don't understand why Europeans throw out this old furniture and go buy IKEA instead. In my parents' house, we have centuries-old furniture, and we still use it. When I get married, I'll take some with me.' Then she went to Venice and married her boyfriend. He had flown over from the States with a romantic notion. 'We'll take the train from Budapest to Venice!' he said. Juliana was surprised that Americans thought Budapest and Venice were just a quick train ride apart. Perhaps like the distance from Budapest to Bratislava was for her.

Jackie went back to the warm, sticky South, to her parents' large house, where there were old armoires from times of slavery, and outside, there was a garden with magnolias under which she had taken pictures of herself long ago. She packed a few pieces of furniture and followed her husband. Jackie, with the apple in her fridge. Jackie, who was still paying for art school. Jackie, who brought her lunch in a plastic container and heated it up in the microwave in the university cafeteria. She had budgeted her scholarship to the day. Every day she ate spaghetti, and she picked up extra ketchup packets at McDonald's. 'Do you know what we ordered after the ceremony? Spaghetti!' she wrote from Venice. 'I splattered tomato sauce on my dress on purpose. Awesome, beautiful!'

Jackie, who cut her hair again before going to Venice. And took pictures of herself again. Juliana and Cristina helped her. She grabbed scissors, dull scissors she found at the back of a drawer. 'Oh, I didn't know I had scissors!' Cristina helped her cut the back and level the front. Hair was falling to the ground, and Juliana was supposed to document each phase. Instead of looking into the camera, she kept looking at Jackie in the mirror. Awesome, beautiful!

Take My Hand, Take My Whole Life Too

'Is anyone around here born in Hungary?' While the foam was settling on the beer, the bartender was pouring pálinka into shotglasses. Then he finished pouring the beer and set it in front of Juliana. 'Almost from Hungary,' she shouted in response to his question so that he could hear her over the noise. He scoffed and slammed five shot glasses on the counter, handing the pálinka to a group of Brits. A group of Frenchmen wanted to pay, and a couple of Japanese women were looking for a bathroom.

Once more around the wobbly table. 'They hate us here,' she said to her colleagues. She told them about the conversation at the bar. In response to the accusation that no one at the bar was from Hungary, she told the bartender that she was from a neighbouring country. Then she took a different tack. It was supposed to be funny. 'So I said that we were the ones boosting the Hungarian economy,' which pissed him off even more. 'Not my economy!' Over her beer, Juliana pondered which economy might be his.

Later on, she added up her regular expenses in her head, a personal economics inventory. She lived in an apartment in the centre of town. When she signed her lease, the letterhead had the name of some Irish woman in Dublin. She shopped for clothes in Zara, H&M, Mango, Pull and Bear, and New Yorker. Once in a while she bought some accessory of

Hungarian design, a bag or a piece of jewellery. When she needed something for the apartment, she got on the metro and went to IKEA. Or she wrote an email to the agency and they brought it there. She ate her lunches at a Chinese restaurant, in Hari Krishna, or in a cafeteria under the business centre. She attended a university that was going to give her a diploma from the University of the State of New York. She didn't even have to cross the Atlantic. Only the water she drank and the air she breathed were local. Oh, and she bought Hungarian smoked sheep cheese, which she secretly thought was the best in the Visegrad region.

She spent a moment thinking about whether she had any Hungarian friends. 'Do you have any Hungarian friends?' the Hungarian receptionist at the university asked her. A man buttoned up in a comical livery in every weather. He said they didn't get paid much. He was different, he didn't do crossword puzzles or watch TV series. He studied English, took an interest in the students, and wanted to study at the university. He didn't know what yet, but he wanted to. He showed her a special award that the student union had given him for his work: 'the nicest employee of the year'. 'What's going on outside?' Juliana asked him. Something was about to happen in front of the cathedral; the square was blocked off by barricades, things were being carried, a podium was being built. 'It is a big Hungarian day tomorrow. When the king of Hungary . . .' The receptionist made an expansive gesture with his arms meant to express the relationship of the king to his country from the Balkans to the Tatras.

Juliana said thank you and walked out. She went back to the cathedral and watched. Men carrying some kind of an adorned box were walking between the barricades. They walked slowly; the box must have been heavy or highly esteemed, it wouldn't have been appropriate to rush with it. The men were wearing jeans and work shirts. According to the receptionist, the box contained the remains of St. Stephen. A hand with a ring set on velvet.

The square was lined with establishments where life didn't stop on account of a few bones. Above one outdoor seating area the light bulbs were on even during the day—*Take my hand, take my whole life too* . . . Invisible speakers played Elvis. That old swaying melody accompanied the box on the way to the cathedral. People were laughing on the outdoor terraces and flashing their drinks. The square was empty, and the men, now visibly bent under the weight of the box, looked as if they were bringing the arc. It was so beautiful that Juliana went weak at the knees. She knelt on the cobblestones, and to complete the gesture she crossed herself, because kneeling made no sense on its own.

An older woman leaned on her crutch and crossed herself too. Two Japanese tourists put their hands together with a camera and indicated a bow. Smiling, they approached Juliana and asked her about the meaning of the box and the holiday. 'It's an important day for Hungarians, Slovaks, and everyone who lived here when our king established the Kingdom of Hungary. These are his bones. His hand, his ring.' The Japanese women nodded and waved around their thick guide to Central Europe. They said they hadn't read about it in the book. 'The book needs to be updated,' Juliana said, laughing with them. Bobbing their heads to indicate goodbye, they left for the California Coffee Company at the corner of the square. From there, they watched the box enter the Basilica of St. Stephen.

She bought two cups of coffee and two pieces of strudel at the school snack bar. She told the receptionist, who was her only Hungarian acquaintance, her theory about how it was a shared holiday of all Central Europeans. 'The university should do something . . . We bike on Earth Day, we buy toys for a Christmas charity drive, but what about this holiday? We got a mass email to "avoid possible protests!" ' The employee of the year concurred: 'Foreign students should not go downtown today.' He dusted the sugar off his livery and proposed that St. Stephen at least deserved a statue. 'Or a song . . .' They tossed their paper trays into the recycle bin. 'A musical,' he said. 'The King', she suggested a title.

Self-Loves

It was a strange sound. Juliana had never heard a fire alarm before. She opened her eyes; the ceiling was very close to her bunk bed. She sat up, and in a few seconds she made sense of the events that had been disordered by the logic of dreams. It was nighttime. She was at a hostel in Newcastle. There were five other people in the room. All of them were already standing by their beds and packing up some things. So she climbed down the ladder. She didn't know what to do. She had never experienced a fire alarm before. She put on her shoes and picked up her purse. Someone said 'Good morning' with sarcasm and an accent. She didn't know anyone in the room. New people came in during the three nights she had been there. The other night she had seen a tall Black guy on the lower bunk; in the morning a small Asian-looking woman was sleeping there, snoring loudly. Now a young man was sitting on the bed, quietly cursing in Italian, and wearing very ugly pyjamas. The room didn't have a chair, a table, or a closet. Only three bunk beds and a mirror that twisted people's figures into bizarre shapes.

The sound stopped. The alarm was over. No one said anything. Her roommates headed back to their beds. Juliana set down her purse, which she otherwise always kept with her—in the bathroom she hung it on the doorknob, in the shower she hung it on a hook on the door, and when she cooked in the shared kitchenette, she had it slung over her shoulder. Now she left her purse covered with her pillow and walked out into the hallway. 'Sorry, someone pulled the alarm!' a voice yelled up the stairs from reception. She had never seen the man before. Maybe he didn't even work there.

She wanted to spend her day off touring the town. She had come for a two-day conference, plus an extra day. But she couldn't fall back asleep. Her heart was racing, fired up by the false alarm. The room was cold; it could have used a little bit of fire. She listened to what her bunkmates were doing. Whether they had fallen asleep again. She listened to them breathe. The guy beneath her kept stirring and moaning. At first she thought that his heart was racing too, he couldn't sleep, and had plans in the morning. Then she felt the bed shaking rhythmically. She tried to shake the persistent thought that the man who had been cursing in Italian was engaging in such an activity in a room with five people who had only recently gone to bed. The shaking woke her up completely. She couldn't decide whether to be quietly embarrassed into her pillow, or to sit up in her bed in protest, dangle her feet over the edge, climb down, and perhaps close the window. Before she made up her mind, she fell asleep. The masturbating Italian rocked her and the whole metal bunk bed to sleep.

In the morning, as her toast came popping out of the toaster, she remembered her dreams. In her dream she was pressing up against someone's body to get warm. It was so pleasant that in the morning the water in the shower seemed a little more bearably tepid. She set out into the drizzly, foggy weather, to see the town. The conference had fallen on the two sunny days. At least she got to go outside during lunch break, turn her face towards the sun, and light a cigarette. One of the waiters smoked alongside her, no one else. 'Hi! Last smokers on Earth,' she said.

When she woke up, first she looked at the fire alarm on the wall, now innocuous, and then she looked at the window. The fog was so thick, it was as though someone had closed the blinds. Juliana was sitting in an air-conditioned bus on her way to a lookout spot on the outskirts of town. In a brochure at the hostel she found ideas on how to spend the few hours before her return flight. She decided to go see the angel statue, the largest outdoor sculpture in Britain. As she stood beneath the statue, she broke down in tears. The fog covered the statue completely. She stood under its legs, and leaned her head back to try to see something. A huge body with outstretched arms towered over her. The sculpture stood on a coal mine, buried deep into a former mine shaft, one of many in the mining region near Newcastle. That was what the plaque by the sculpture said.

Victory to the working class! A poster with the motto hung on the facade of the Museum of Modern Art. Entry was free. A video ran on a loop in a darkened room. Juliana stood in the doorway and waited for the bench in front of the screen to empty. On the screen there was a woman standing by a river in India. The author of the video art did nothing but stand there and look into the river. Chunks of objects, branches, and trash floated in the muddy water. The video ended abruptly, like a torn film strip. The screen went dark, and when the loop came back on, the woman who had been sitting under the screen was gone.

Juliana sat down to watch the video from the beginning. As she sat there, she stopped focusing on the woman by the swollen river, and felt warmth. It was coming from the bench where people had been taking turns all day. A warm impression of rear ends. For a moment she stopped feeling cold. She wondered whether she should get up and find the woman who had sat there before her. Talk to her at the souvenir shop, ask her to take a picture with the panorama of the town, and perhaps invite her for a coffee at the restaurant on the top floor. 'Restaurants are always on the top floor. We don't need to look for a map of the building,' she'd say. 'Have you ever experienced a fire alarm?' They could make a sarcastic video together, in which they'd take turns standing for 10 minutes on the bank of the river Tyne, which had nothing floating in it except for the reflection of the revitalized silhouette of town. Awesome, beautiful, she remembered. But then she stayed put, enjoying a little private warmth on the bench while the loop ran two more times.

I Think I'm Dying

Juliana was sitting in a waiting room, holding Jackie's hand— her fingers were ice cold. Juliana rubbed them, held them in her hand, and asked for the hundredth time: 'OK?' Jackie just nodded. People waiting for the ER were sitting all around them. An old gentleman, who was whimpering in pain while someone helped him to the bathroom where he probably wasn't able to pee, came back to the bench. A lady was changing her bandage. A bloody, rumpled bandage on her hand kept soaking through. Then two cops brought in a man who kept grimacing. He reeked of something that reminded Juliana of Christmas. Diava, polishing furniture. Okena, glass cleaning. And something for cleaning tiles. The man swung at the air, and the bandage flew off the woman's hand. The old gentleman yelped and peed himself. Only Jackie kept looking ahead and taking deep breaths. She concentrated on calming herself down. 'Get up, let's walk around a bit!' Juliana tugged on her to get her to move. She went faster, kept speeding up, forced Jackie to run. Jackie needed to stop thinking about breathing; if she ran, she'd stop observing herself.

Juliana knew it would work. For over a year she had been running regularly at the gym. Especially on days when she woke up with a feeling that she was behind on everything. She knew it was only stress deposited in her body like lime scale in an electric teakettle. It needed to be dissolved and sweated out. After 15 minutes of running, the stiff body warmed up, then her breathing evened; after 20 minutes she knew who she was and what she was doing there; and after half an hour her priorities shifted and she knew that everything was as it was supposed to be. She laughed at the stressed-out students sitting behind desks at the library as if they were in a factory. When the time came again, she went running, lifted weights, did sit-ups, hung on the wall bars, boxed a punching bag. Usually, she was accompanied by the gazes of three guys from the Caucasian republics.

'They were at the gym again. You know, the unibrows,' she said as they ran along the ER hallway. That had to make Jackie laugh. She needed to remember that there were other mindboggling things in the world. They called them the unibrows. Their eyebrows were joined in the middle, so that whenever they were surprised or tried to suggest going out for coffee, their eyebrows made a Mexican wave. They'd rise on one end and fall on the other. They went to the school gym almost daily. Always together. 'Adin, dva, tri!' they counted out loud in Russian, a language that connected them across the Caucasus. As they counted, they made jerky movements, the likes of which she remembered from warm-ups at elementary school.

The last time it happened, she couldn't keep watching it any more and went over to tell them to stop flailing about lest they tear a tendon. They immediately invited her for coffee. That had to make Jackie laugh. So much had happened. Juliana had planned to tell her about it over a bottle of wine. And over sardines with half an apple. She bought a can of sardines and a kilo of tiny green apples in preparation for Jackie's visit. They were running back when a door opened and someone told them to stop running. A nurse called them in. She sent Juliana out to the hallway, took one look at Jackie, and asked her what was wrong with her in English. 'I think I'm dying,' Jackie said, completely serious.

It all started with a text message from Jackie, in which she let Juliana know that she'd be coming the next day on a train from Venice and she wanted to spend the night. Juliana was looking forward to it—she cleaned, cooked, bought flowers at the market. Jackie came and didn't even notice the flowers. 'I'm divorced,' she said in the doorway. She was some 20 pounds lighter than when Juliana had seen her off to the States. She kept making herself tea in the middle of the night. She drank beer from a can at all hours. In the morning, she'd take a bite of bread, but wouldn't finish a single slice. She'd cover the plate, saying she was saving it for later. During the day she'd go to the library. She said she was preparing a proposal for a doctoral project. She wanted to go back to school. She wanted to stay in Europe. She'd be writing, and all of a sudden tears would stream down her face. She couldn't see the computer screen any more. She couldn't concentrate on books. Juliana never found out what actually happened. 'Nothing, nothing actually happened,' Jackie said. Suddenly she couldn't be married any more. She just couldn't do it.

'There's nothing wrong with you. You just need a new man,' the doctor said, laughing and patting Jackie on the back. He took her blood pressure, listened to her heart and lungs, checked her throat. He pressed on her stomach. He looked over her hands. He shook her head. She was supposed to follow his finger with her eyes. Then he sent her home. It's nothing. Divorce is not an ailment. You should rest. Jackie couldn't rest. From the metro she saw a poster on the pavement advertising the *Bodies* exhibit. The poster showed a body dissected so that the mass of muscles gave the impression of being deep in thought. The metro door opened, and a crowd rushed through the middle of the poster. They hurried towards the escalator, stepping on the picture. Jackie walked around the poster. In Venice she had gone to places she had visited with her new husband. She told herself she'd send him a postcard from every place they had been together. Just a blank postcard. 'That seems inadequate . . . And sad,' a man she met on the train said to her. 'What should I do then?' 'Stab him with a knife,' he said. He was a married barrister. 'I'll get you out of it.' He winked at her and handed her his card.

'I'm divorced,' she said when Juliana opened the door. She had gotten married. And once she had a thick band with his name on her finger, he didn't want her any more. As if he had lost interest. They were in his town, lived in his apartment, got together with his friends, talked about his work and his problems. All she had brought with her was her antique furniture. She was looking for work and taking cooking classes online. The more time she spent there, the more she became a piece of furniture. A termite-laden armoire. The last few months she had been with him, something started to happen to her body, and she got terrible acne on her cheeks. She looked at her cheeks in the mirror, they looked like the surface of the moon. Her nails were covered in white spots. Her belly retained water, she was bloated, her clothes were too tight. She thought it could be hormones. The opposite of pregnancy. He would lie down next to her, take a sip of tea, and fall asleep. With his back to her, turned the other away, gone. She promised herself not to ask him any questions. To let him rest. She listened to him breathe. She loved him so much. She wanted to give him all the time in the world to deal with whatever he was dealing with. As she was falling asleep, she told herself that it was just her imagination. It was nothing serious. He was tired. He was her husband and he was tired. That was all.

'I'm sorry. I'm so sorry. I don't have feelings for you any more. I'm sorry. I can't help it. What are we going to do? I'm not seeing anyone else. I just want to be alone. I'm sorry. I'm really sorry. My sincerest apologies,' he said one day at dinner. She had told him that she could make sushi; all he needed to do was pick up some seaweed at the Korean store on his way home. He asked her to meet him in town at a Japanese restaurant. She didn't finish her dinner. The sushi came to life in her mouth and started to wiggle in her stomach. She got up and went home. He let her go. She took a taxi, told the driver the address, and watched her own face in the rearview mirror. It reminded her of a porcelain mask from Venice they had brought back from their honeymoon. It frightened her every time she went to the bathroom at night. Its eyes gleamed. In the strips of light from the street lamps she saw her pupils. They were huge. They stayed that way all week. As if she had just gone bungee jumping.

'I'm getting a divorce,' she told her parents. Things weren't finalized yet, and the tense of the sentence suggested that there might be a way back. 'It's really over. I mean, I'm sorry, I just want it to be clear,' he called. So that she wouldn't come back from her parents' with an attempt at reconciliation. With a new hairdo and a new dress. Perhaps with new furniture as well. From then on she spoke about it as a done deal. While she was visiting her parents, she went to see New Orleans. She had coffee on the river island. There was only one subway stop there, houses in ruins, and no one but old people walking down the streets. They must have been the only ones who didn't have the strength to move elsewhere.

She should sketch. Everyone was telling her to express herself. To paint, since that used to be her favourite thing to do. She couldn't even unscrew the lid off a tube of paint. Nor sharpen a pencil. She couldn't hold onto a charcoal. The camera was his, it stayed there. Her sister took her to a concert, where they head banged like in the old days. 'Oh, the breakups I've been through!' she said. Jackie's sister had set up a profile on some dating site, and since then she had broken up countless times. Jackie felt like her sister just sat around, danced, and drank wine. She was celebrating another breakup, her divorce. She suggested that Jackie set up her own profile. 'You'll see, you'll learn to like it. Don't you think it's at least a little sweet? Sweet, sweet pain! Enjoy it!'

'I'm divorced,' she said to Juliana. She had left her artwork portfolio at her parents'. Juliana watched her from behind the flowers on the table. At the spa she had seen Jackie's protruding ribs, her sagging butt, and her skin, which had lost all elasticity. She had seen her walking on the stone floor of the Turkish bath in nothing but flip-flops. Jackie sat down on the pool steps, propped up her chin with her hand, and stared at the surface of the water. Juliana handed her a Baedeker so she'd come up with something to do every day. She had to go somewhere and then tell Juliana what she had seen. She came back with red eyes and described the grave of a Turkish soldier on the Buda side. Or the interior of a church in the 8th district where there was a mummy behind glass. She sent her husband a postcard with the hand of St. Stephen. Then she went to the *Bodies* exhibit.

They went to a spa together, Tuesday was women-only day. The building of the Rudás spa was dilapidated. Anyone who didn't know it, would pass by and barely notice it. It was as though the sulphur springs had dissected the building. Inside, everything was run down as well. The dressing rooms had wobbly doors that opened with scratched up key cards. But in the main atrium above the pool there was a cupola with coloured windows that let in magical strips of light. The clock on the wall was fogged up, you couldn't see the numbers. Juliana was standing in the pool, up to her neck in the water, and saw Jackie coming. She sat on the stairs for a while. She watched the water, then the colourful glass. Then she walked down the steps and submerged herself. According to a sign on the wall, the water was the exact temperature of the human body. 'Who would have thought we're so hot on the inside!' she said.

After Jackie came back from the exhibit of dissected bodies, she had trouble breathing. She washed the dishes.

Then she went to look at herself in the mirror. She checked her pupils. She sat down in the kitchen, but she couldn't stand the clock ticking. It was as if something were coming, but she didn't know what. It was coming from far away, and it was almost there. She drank something. She opened a window. She unbuttoned the top button of her jeans. She took off her T-shirt so it wouldn't be making her uncomfortable. She concentrated on breathing. Juliana found her with her head between her knees, breathing deeply. 'I think I'm dying,' she said.

Juliana had seen the emergency numbers posted in the elevator. She knew how to say police in Hungarian, and between ambulance and fire she had a 50/50 chance of picking the right number. By the time they connected her to someone who spoke English, Jackie was just staring into space and gripping the backrest of a chair. She kept breathing, and tears streamed down her cheeks. 'I'm dying, I'm dying,' she kept saying. The woman on the telephone told Juliana to take a taxi and bring the patient to the ER. Jackie kept looking at herself in the rearview mirror. 'We should let him know I'm dying. He should know. He should know about it.'

Juliana didn't want to make light of it, but she knew that feeling and she also knew that they'd be laughing about it the next day. She had never had such a strong anxiety attack, but one time when she was overworked, she walked out of a class and outside the door she collapsed into an armchair. She started to breathe and felt death approaching. The elevator door dinged, death got off, and walked down the hallway towards her. She asked her 'How are you?,' went on without waiting for an answer, and closed her office door. Holding on to the walls and the banister, Juliana walked down to the school doctor. She banged on the door, counting her inhalations and exhalations, and when the nurse shouted 'Wait!' she turned the door knob and barged in. A patient immediately let her go ahead when she said: 'I think I'm dying!'

The doctor and the nurse exchanged glances.

Jackie asked Juliana if she could sleep in her bed. She was still a bit slow and confused. Juliana went to take a shower to give her time to lie down. The hot water relaxed her. She promised herself that she'd make herself tea and turn her back to Jackie like her husband. She promised herself that she'd fall asleep immediately. When she came out of the bathroom, Jackie was already asleep. Her breathing was finally just right; deep, regular, calm. Her hair had a light scent of sulphur from the baths. The next day she met Cristina: 'I would have definitely called the fire department by mistake!' She laughed. 'Don't worry, we'll find you a guy, you'll be fine.'

She found a postcard in her postbox. Jackie was saying hi from Sarajevo. She was inviting Juliana to visit her in her apartment with a huge terrace with a view of the mountains surrounding the town. Jackie quickly found friends there. She found a job. Nothing to do with art. She was learning Bosnian. For the time being, she was able to name all of the white pastries made from phyllo dough: durek, dolma, zeljanica, baklava. She gained weight. She had bought the postcard for her ex, but then she felt like writing a few sentences on it. After all, they had never been to Sarajevo together. She sent it to

Juliana. She'd have to come to the terrace! It was where she and her friends and colleagues went to smoke. Cheap cigarettes, great coffee. Mosques and churches. Traces of a great tragedy here and there. Such as shrapnel holes in the stucco of the houses by the river. The city had recovered. 'Old decommissioned Czechoslovak trams ride around here!' she wrote. It sufficed for her as a temporary happy ending.

Trianon–Delta

TRIANON

'How do you feel? How are you?' she asked. It was our third breakfast together. The sun was shining through an aquarium onto the table. A bowl of tuna spread I brought was sitting there. I didn't know how to answer. *Here's fresh olive bread. Here's butter to go with it. How are you?*

The sound of keys outside the door startled me. I tried to decide between hiding in the closet, under the bed, or on the window ledge. What would her boyfriend think, what would he say, what would he do? Should I go have a beer with him and talk it over? I could still just be a friend who was having breakfast with her after a night of movies and talking about guys.

'He'd probably ask me how my night was. And he'd hope you enjoyed it too,' she said without any sign of panic. A heroine, who makes terrible filtered coffee and gives kisses at the door. Kiss! She has empty wrappers in the fridge. The ham is curled up like a message in a bottle, dry at the edges. Yet she also has a jar of Ukrainian caviar. Every time I'm with her I forget that I'm vegetarian. We eat salami and fish.

My insides are like an empty fridge. My heart is a piece of old ham with hardened red edges. I weigh 128 lbs. at 5'9'. I can't remember the last time I was so thin. Perhaps after a stay in Starý Smokovec. Respiratory diseases. When I got there, I was too proud to eat hot dogs. By the time I was leaving, I was no longer picky and spoilt. I ate fatty chunks of meat, and hot dogs were my favourite breakfast delicacy. Whenever I eat hot dogs now, my body is flooded with pleasant feelings. That'll never go away. I must write the truth—favourite food: hot dogs.

'You'll be much more at ease! You'll be a more interesting person,' she said about my recent breakup. For a few months I didn't sleep well. Budapest might be the town with the most ambulances and fire trucks flying by. It must be the most unfortunate metropolis in Europe. Every single siren woke me up. She said: 'You look like you came from a concentration camp. Are you sure you're not Jewish? You look Jewish. You should claim it. It would make you all the more interesting.'

I'm 28 years old, freshly single, 128 pounds, a smoker, maybe Jewish. With a high alcohol tolerance. A passable cook, although my figure doesn't currently show it. I like to exercise, I lift weights. I left my last relationship with nothing but a pair of blue speakers and a muffin pan from IKEA.

———

We each have a role. I am the storyteller. She is the muse. She's Romanian. She looks like a Gypsy. A beautiful Gypsy. She says that if it gave her more cachet in the academic world, she'd gladly say she's a Gypsy. She'd invent a whole childhood under Ceauçescu, she'd invent a history of Romania, she'd even invent a whole new state on the map of Europe. It's so easy.

We can be whoever we want to be. In the States, she frightened a cashier, a simple woman from the prairie, when she pulled out her debit card issued by the Bank of Transylvania.

What do I actually know about her? She went from being a conservative to the left. I'm living proof of her newfound social sympathy. She considers herself a feminist. She tries to be active, useful. In stereotypical fashion, she doesn't cook. If she ever does, it's an act of hysteria, in which she puts together duck, canned fruit, and leftover sparkling wine. Moreover, she doesn't like to do the dishes. She likes to wear clothes from second-hand stores. Unique and retro. Who cares about fashion?

'Look!' She dragged me behind a fitting room curtain, pulled up the dress she was trying on, and showed me her thigh covered in cellulite. I looked at her reflection in the mirror and honestly said: 'You look great!' She does look great. She left the second-hand store in a white summer dress, pushing a bicycle. I walked behind her and kept looking to see if other people were seeing how beautiful she looked in her new dress. I didn't have the courage to hold her hand.

I'm a storyteller. I give words. She is a heroine. She gives actions and words and gestures. I walk a step behind her, like a Gypsy woman, in awe: this is my girlfriend. This is my new love! We're at school together. We're together.

'It's high time for us to exchange our private email addresses,' she said over Skype. She wants me to send her an email with a detailed description of my recent trip to Sarajevo. She's in Bucharest right now, and she wants to read me, if nothing else.

She submitted an application for a new passport. I wanted to see the photo she was going to have in it, and to read what the little booklet said about her. *Hair colour? Material? Eye colour? Describe your fingerprints! Blushing?* I can't help it, I blush. 'They say it's a skin issue. Either it's too thin, or too pale.' (I have a thing for explaining phenomena.) Luckily, she has olive skin. I bet she wouldn't blush even if she had thin, pale skin. She's brave. Clever. And very rational. Sometimes I think she's too cool. And yet, when she's pressed up against me, she's soft and hot. I want to put on lipstick and press my lips onto a page of her new passport. Kiss!

I wrote her that I almost had a panic attack when I opened my school email account and realized that it was full of unread messages. The counter in the upper right corner showed critical. I hadn't checked that email for some time. She wrote me back something about things that are important, and about those that aren't. She told me to do the things that make me happy, and enjoy the things I do.

It sounds like something from a pop-psychology hand-book. It's the kind of sentence we tell other people even though we don't believe it ourselves. They're words that have to be in circulation, putting wind into our Tibetan flags, turning our prayer mills, and making our Feng shui bells ring. The words don't mean anything, it's dead language. It's like singing in Sanskrit at a yoga class. Yet they act as a blessing. They're also gentle commands. As I was leaving my ex, he put 'don't worry, be happy' as his Facebook status. A tiny prayer, mumbled by 365 of his friends.

She was asking the same of me. For me to simply be happy. All of a sudden, just like that. What's the appropriate amount of time for grieving? How long can I annoy people around me by dressing in black? When I got undressed and walked across the room, it was the first time I didn't blush. But it was only because I had a thin black film on that had permeated my skin. Like in the fairy tale—she came up to him half-naked-half-dressed, like the soldier with a uniform painted on his naked body, like the naked lady on a horse, wrapped only in her long hair. I lay next to her on the couch.

I decided to use love as my main organizing force. It's a force that helps people come to terms with small annoyances such as opening emails and responding to them. I clicked on them one after another, the way one opens a forgotten advent calendar.

<hr />

I kept thinking about order. About the geometry of love. I had become one of the vertices of a love triangle. Did logic demand that I also sleep with her boyfriend? Math and abstraction had never been my thing. I should ask my roommate. Oh, not in that sense! Not for her to join us! She's good with numbers. When she came back from an internship at Oxford, she figured out that the energy usage records had been neglected, said 'What a mess!' and started to count. The result was an organized, neat ledger with an underlined answer. She's religious. Arithmetic can only work in a world where a great force holds things together.

But I promised myself not to drag any more characters into this story. It should be only about her. She's been gone for some time. We're in touch via email and Skype. In electronic touch. Ones and zeroes. 'So you're still a fan of human contact?' she asked, laughing. Some time ago she suggested that I get a vibrator. I blushed. She said that her ex had written her once to come get hers or he was going to throw it out. I was outraged by the idea of *it* rolling around in the trash. *It's almost human, isn't it?*

'I don't want this modern relationship!' my ex had written in our last email exchange. After I had disintegrated into ones and zeroes and sent myself via email. I practically teleported myself. And still it wasn't enough. No wonder that a vibrator can't replace a penis. One is to the other like a penis is to a phallus. It's just a promise. So he stayed there and I stayed here. Bratislava–Budapest. But my here is still trembling, vibrating.

I'm counting the days until her return. To make the time go by faster, I accepted an invitation to a date. With a colleague from Sarajevo. I'm going out to breathe smoke and drink bad wine. While I'm at it, I'll send her a text message.

———

She hasn't replied yet and she's ignoring my green status on Skype. Both inboxes are empty. What do I actually know about her? A wave of embarrassment came over me when I realized that after three years of smoking in the courtyard and sitting around pubs with our classmates together, and even after our timid dating, I didn't know that much about her. Perhaps she doesn't deserve a whole book to herself.

I knew so many little things about him! Recently, when I was locking my laptop to the library railing, I recalled how much I used to love to wash his clothes. I liked how they smelt when they were dirty, and I also loved their fresh scent when they were clean. I could sell any old laundry detergent! 'You're as thin as a laptop. You should start to eat more!' she said with her arm around my waist. She looked like she was covered with a thin layer of pudding. Her hair was as straight as spaghetti, and her face was the colour of café latte. I gulped.

I quickly turned on my computer and asked her what she liked to eat and what she didn't. The only things she didn't want were onions and beans. I could have tossed everything else into a large pot and served it for lunch when she came back. I knew I could burn the food and she wouldn't mind. 'Let's have a sandwich instead,' she'd say. I appreciate how she doesn't care about unimportant things. Like food. I looked at recipes with the notion that I could make anything, and that filled me with joy and freedom. *No to gourmet cooking from* Apetite *magazine*! And more importantly, *No to time at IKEA*!

He and I. We were standing in the middle of the kitchen section when I realized that we might not be a good couple. That hadn't occurred to me before. All of a sudden it started to take shape, until it turned into a clear statement: *He worries about unimportant things*! I was ashamed of this thought, which quickly started to consume everything around us. It dropped us naked and pitiful in the middle of IKEA. We looked totally out of place in every section, we didn't buy anything but caviar paste, and then security ran us out of home paradise. They were closing. How prosaic.

We left our matching halves in the kitchen section. We didn't have disagreements over colours or shapes. I dare say, we shared a good taste. We unequivocally agreed on a built-in refrigerator for two. Practical, uncluttered. I unrolled a piece of dried out ham from her fridge and spread caviar on it. Meat with fish roe. The morning coffee was standing on the counter, cold. Ants could ice skate on it. 'Ants can ice skate on this coffee,' I said to her. Nothing had ever sounded so strange.

Her apartment had great natural light. It was light and airy. The floors were cold, but when her parents came to visit, they put insulation around all the windows so that cold air wouldn't get in. She didn't mind. She didn't care. The apartment had no balcony, only a window above the sink, therefore some of the cigarette smoke permanently hung above the kitchen table. She didn't object. She didn't even notice. There was a double bed. 'It's not big enough for two,' she said. So she dragged another person into it. No problem. She looked calm. Perhaps she couldn't count either.

Every time I got worried about gossip, she said: 'Don't worry about unimportant things!' *Don't worry, be happy.* So I tried it. I started by sliding my feet into her boyfriend's slippers and walking around the apartment with his cup. The cup had his name on it and my lipstick. It was a good start to not worrying about unimportant things.

———

Dust particles, sharp as a broken mirror, could scratch the surfaces of machines and damage their internal parts if they got sucked in. Hurricanes and falling governments—literally falling from the sky—all the forces of nature were set in motion to prevent us from meeting again.

Her flight from Bucharest was cancelled, so I had to postpone my plans for making her lunch, having a glass of wine with her in the courtyard of a beautiful place, and then perhaps kissing her too-small breasts. My plans were modest. I couldn't do more because of my period. As I said, all the forces of nature . . .

During dinner at a Bangladeshi restaurant, which was so tiny it felt like being stuck in an elevator, my colleague from Sarajevo explained to me how a cloud from an exploded volcano on Iceland works. He continued with why the sky appears blue, and why water looks as though it's reflecting the sky. It was all an illusion.

He couldn't have surprised me less. I've never trusted the reality of things. I had to go through a breakup in order to realize the existence of love. I'm getting to know its reality in its absence. Yet there I was, faced with the same problem. I was peeling away my feelings for her, one after another, and I tried to give them exact names—respect, trust, friendship—

only to confirm the emptiness under the layers, the lack of love.

What if all she feels for me is sympathy? I asked myself. Isn't that exactly what love is? Doesn't she keep asking me how I'm doing? Doesn't she keep an eye on whether I'm eating? Doesn't she compliment me? Doesn't she write me long, detailed emails? Doesn't she ask me out on dates? Doesn't she wait for me outside my classroom, and send me messages if I disappear without making plans with her for the evening? Isn't she fabulous? Could some pitiful cloud of volcanic dust prevent her from coming to Budapest to eat, drink, and make love with me?

After a long time I turned on my Slovak cell phone and it said 'Welcome to Hungary!' In a funny way it reminded me of where I was. She made it to Budapest after an 18-hour train ride. Other people on the train were traveling from Istanbul all the way to Stockholm. I said that now it made sense why there was a murder on the Orient Express. The shaking of the train stayed with her for several days.

In the meantime, her boyfriend had a wisdom tooth pulled; his cheek was swollen, he could barely eat or sleep. It seemed as though we had traded places: I was sleeping passably well, with only occasional nightmares, and I was gaining weight. 'Yeah, I can see it on your cheeks,' she said. My cheeks were a bit more full. My school project started to come together. Food was once more varied and tasty. The weather was good most of the time, and when it wasn't, I didn't mind.

In midday light she was more beautiful than ever. We exchanged compliments and gifts. It was high noon, and we were sitting on the terrace, drinking a late morning coffee. The cathedral bell rang, and she said 'Ouch!' For a while her tongue searched around her mouth, and then she pulled out a piece of tooth with her fingers. It looked like a piece of a peanut: too yellow for being a normal tooth. True, she smokes a lot.

'It's got to be because we're sharing an apartment, that's why we both have issues with teeth. I can't think of anything else we have in common,' she said, summing up her and his tooth incidents. I realized that we both live with the ghosts of men. Mine shows up in a dream in the morning and turns it into a nightmare. Sometimes we just stand there facing each other; he has a new girlfriend by his side—based on my sub-conscious wish she has a big butt or badly bleached hair. Sometimes he's dressed, other times he's naked. One time he was naked and doing high jumps like a Maasai warrior. I often wake up sweaty, and I have to think of a good reason to get out of bed and take part in the flow of the world. Her boyfriend wanders around the apartment absently, watches football, and talks about Marxism.

She sent a message that I should join them, have a beer with them. *Not a chance*, I told myself. But then I remembered that this is my story. I felt a responsibility. How could I let the storyteller chicken out and stay home? What would happen to the story if I didn't go out for the beer? A real hero would buy flowers at the corner and walk in with a bouquet of fresh tulips with such a dizzying scent that it would scare off her boyfriend. But I just walked out of the building, fumbled around my wallet, pulled out a few coins, and after a few steps I tossed them into a Cola cup to a man who looked like he worked at the belfry of Notre Dame.

She and I drank beer. He couldn't because of his tooth. Sipping lemonade, he talked about Marxism. That was when I started to like him. I couldn't stand his fake American accent. To be honest, I secretly thought that she had a bad taste in guys. But at that moment he seemed OK. He asked about my plans for the future, and said that he'd be glad to go out for a beer with me when he got better. I suspect he also liked me.

'Alex McQueen has died! Did you know?' I knew. I got that message from her after returning to Budapest. The only reason I knew this bit of celebrity gossip was because of a magazine I had flipped through on the bus between Bratislava and Budapest. She was reading the same book I was. It was a paperback by Magda Szabó. English translations of Hungarian literature were limited, and we wanted to get to know the local soul. Perhaps it was a coincidence that we both reached for the same book cover at the bookstore, attracted by the same colours and shapes.

The first time she woke up at my place, she had had a dream about a tooth. I knew from my grandmother that it was a bad omen. Oral tradition of explaining bad omens: muddy water, teeth, and babies. 'It's just because I live on the street where you go to the dentist,' I said. I decided to dispel the bad omen.

'Do you think it's time we started to kiss in public?' she asked. To tell the truth, I had been thinking about it as we walked up the stairs to the castle. There was only a handful of people there, and the stern pale face of the moon. I waited until we got to the top. The view of the Pest side was postcard-beautiful. Blinking lights, the hypnotic pull of traffic, and again the moon, now hanging over the scene, expressionless. We crossed the castle square and watched the shimmering lights of the Buda side. There was no one around. The air was full of waxy spring scents: 'Like in Proust!' she said. I didn't kiss her and she didn't kiss me.

A sign said 'Danger, watch out!' We joined some teenagers who were sitting with their feet dangling over a tunnel with yellow trams disappearing into it. We watched the town. The moon was staring at us. It looked like the Skype icon 'smirk'. A full face of a smirker. Her boyfriend was watching football at a pub near the house. My ex was somewhere, I had lost sight of him, and his contours coalesced with the outlines of his new girlfriend. I had seen a few pictures of her on Facebook. No big butt, no peroxide. I knew that he talked in his sleep during a full moon and reached for the body sleeping next to him. Now the Skype moon was showing 'thinking'.

'Shall we go? I still need to write today,' she said, seeing my vacant stare. For the last time I considered pulling her into a dark corner and pressing my lips against hers. But there was a guy urinating in the corner, and a girl was waiting for him nearby.

'What's going on with her? Is she alive?' supposedly the ex of my best friend from elementary school had asked about me. At that time I had ceased to exist for many of my ex's friends. Some even took it as an opportunity to breathe a sigh of relief: *I never actually liked her*! I was hanging by my throat in a closet full of his clothes smelling of detergent that I had bought. The cheapest laundry detergent. 'You bought detergent at Lidl?' he had asked me back then.

'Shall we go honour Alex McQueen's memory?' I suggested. *Everybody cares about fashion*! I went overboard with my perfume and she put on more jewellery than usual. We were sitting in our spot, just the two of us in the courtyard with grapevines. The waiter smiled and made himself scarce for half an hour. 'It's a great loss for women!' I said sarcastically about the article on McQueen's death in a women's magazine. Tiny insects hidden in nearby bushes seemed to be screaming *Kiss, kiss, kiss*! We both lit a cigarette at the same time. I moved my chair closer to her, but I didn't kiss her. Instead I persuaded her to follow me to my room, swearing that my roommate slept hard, so that I could kiss her until I fell into the sheets and let her dream about teeth, muddy water, and babies.

I took an allergy pill. 'Are you taking a morning after pill?' she asked me in the morning, laughing.

———

Her boyfriend called while we were sitting on the terrace of the Italian institute. She had her laptop set up on the small coffee table, and in between our conversation she was messaging her parents via Skype. Then she turned off her computer and her boyfriend on the phone gave up on the idea of joining us. This time he couldn't have a beer because he was getting in shape for the sports day organized by the university. I had also signed up for a race, but I did have a beer. She chose the place, because she was convinced it had the potential for great cappuccinos. Defying all logic, I ordered a beer—lemon-flavored—and I was rightfully disappointed. She had two beautiful frothy cappuccinos, big as soup plates, and the next morning she Skyped me that she couldn't sleep.

The next day there were a lot of emails in support of a protest in front of the Greek Embassy as well as against it. She was always ready to support any cause. Greeks didn't run the terrace, so I decided to go to the cinema instead and see the Hungarian film *Delta*. During the long poetic camera flyovers over the Danube delta, I wondered whether I wasn't just another cause she was supporting. Her little charity project. *Send a text for Haiti*! *Bring canned goods for a shelter*! *Contribute to LGBT rights*! *Watch a documentary about rape*! *Hand out stickers*! *Separate and recycle*!

I was fascinated by her boyfriend's loyalty. He was on the phone, he was in the apartment. After she had lost her keys, they were sharing a set. Even though I can drink more and run faster, time is on his side. Time and also language. They say we only speak in our native tongue. We converse in the others. I wanted to remember who had said that, and slip this nice quote into our coffee table conversation at the Italian institute. I couldn't recall, so we ended up being quiet for a while. Silence sounds different in English than it does in Slovak.

'We live like monks!' my colleague from Sarajevo said. He drank several cappuccinos a day and smoked one cigarette after another. 'You should do some kind of a sport,' I remarked diplomatically in the direction of his gut. 'It's enough that I have sex. I get good quality sex,' he said. He believes in porn democracy and defends having many partners. *If we have distributed consumer goods to the masses, we can't deny them the pleasures that used to be reserved for the privileged.* I blushed and moved my chair away.

'Monks or circus people,' I said. We're nomads who speak the Latin of our times. When the money runs out, we move on. We find new friends. We build new routines. We change lovers. We put the sad face of Picasso's clown at the bottom of our suitcase.

I watched my colleague button and unbutton the top button of his shirt. A gold chain with a cross kept peeking out and disappearing. 'What did you do during those four years in Sarajevo?' I asked him. On a trip to the capital of Bosnia and Herzegovina I had heard about the four years that snipers were lying on the hills surrounding the city. I didn't make it to the museum that had an exhibit about everyday life during the war. Naturally, I was curious about the everyday life. 'Nothing. We did crosswords.' He volleyed back with his own uncomfortable question: 'And how is it with her?' I also dodged. 'She's a very good friend of mine, really!' Matters of love, matters of war.

––––––––

Walking by a second-hand store, I noticed a big heart on a silver chain. The pendant was made of glass, and light refracted in it into all colours of the rainbow. The back was a bit scratched, but that just added to its charm. It was so straightforward that it couldn't even be called kitsch. I had the heart wrapped and put it in my bag. It was high time to start training my heart with the thoughts of a new love.

Because for eight years I had been training it to love him, and it worked. It worked so well that when we broke up, my whole body was asking for him, demanding him by force. In my dreams, at mealtime, in between lines. At one point I swore that I wouldn't let it happen to me again. It wasn't until she wrote that she'd let me stay in her room in Utrecht where she was supposed to transfer for the next semester and she'd share her Erasmus stipend with me, that I realized that she was the one taking on the risk. She didn't mention her boyfriend, and for a moment I forgot about his existence. Not long after that I got a response from the grant committee, in which they told me I'd be on Long Island next year. I'd get my own room and a stipend. I reciprocated her offer: when she comes back from Utrecht, I'll get her a sheet, a plate, and a cup. We'll share the space and the money. My plans were simple and plain like a dorm room.

She held my hand in the taxi, which dropped me off and then took her home, that is, to where she lived with her boyfriend. 'I'll come over some other time, when I'll have more time in the morning to explain to him where I've been. Tomorrow I need to write. And I want to sleep in my own bed.'

I didn't understand. He let us go to a jazz concert together. He let her divide her support evenly between us on sports day. He talks to me, and supposedly he complains that I don't talk to him enough. He knows we sleep together. But she has to go home! When we stayed out past midnight, he called. And they kept making plans together. But she also wanted to go to the West Coast and travel across the States with me (both of us had read the beatniks in school). She said she thought about us, what we'd do on the trip, sleeping in hostels and on beaches. 'The kind of unplanned time like you get during summer vacation.' *Here we're opening a flower shop in Utrecht, here we're standing in front of the Grand Canyon, here we're kissing and both of us are wearing the same dress.* The phone rang. 'I have to sleep at home,' she insisted. She held my hand in the taxi, caressed it, apologized, and offered to pay for the ride.

The glass heart was still wrapped in cellophane at the bottom of my bag. I wondered when the right moment would be to give her the necklace. With a bit of regret I looked at the simplicity of the black dress she had worn to the jazz concert. A shiny heart would be a perfect match for it! We were packed into an auditorium; people stared intently at the podium. Several times she leaned over to me as if to say something, but kissed my ear instead. It looked like an innocent gesture—people either spoke directly into one another's ear, or they shouted to be able to hear. The first time she did it, she caught me off guard—I leaned over to hear what she was saying. I ended up with a wet ear and blushing cheeks.

'I wanted to touch you more, to kiss you more,' she said after the concert. She slipped her hand under my blouse and searched for my tattoo. We knew that we wouldn't be as invisible to people as all those licking and groping couples on escalators, in metro cars, and in Budapest parks. When the phone rang, her hand retreated and she answered the call. *I have to sleep at home.*

———·——

'This is such a romantic city! And we're here alone . . .' one of my classmates said as we were starting our program in Budapest. The city looked gorgeous, it quivered with lights and scents, dotted with barely moving bodies of the homeless, who were transforming into a substance that was fertilizing the hallways of the metro. I searched for the right author whose name would evoke a picture of the city in one breath.

When we finished making love, the room smelt of Bukowski. In her presence, my Spartan-furnished few square feet turned into a teenage den: comic socks on the ground, plates of food on the table, DVDs on the bed, and hormones in the air. 'You're obviously a Protestant! Order, discipline, and guilt,' she analysed me in light of the minimalist decor of the room.

My skin also changed. The same things that predisposed it to dryness, wrinkles, redness, and eczema, could also turn it into a sensitive surface. Connected to a new body, I had to stifle moans with the help of leggings stuffed into my mouth. From beneath the cloth came moans that sounded like the bass in a car with a good stereo. My roommate had the unchanging face of an icon: 'Good morning! I'm going to make hot dogs. How many would you like?'

———

She left in the morning to pick up her passport, which was supposed to be delivered that day. Soon she'd be leaving for Dubrovnik, then on to Bern, Krakow, and then somewhere to Andalusia. Those were her work and vacation plans combined into an idea of summer school. Basically, she was going to be a nomad, drink wine in beautiful places, and have smart conversations with interesting people. I wouldn't try to stop her. Love shouldn't be planned. It should never have its own colour on the calendar.

Whenever I was supposed to be in Bratislava, my ex coloured those days on his calendar. He had different colours for work, sports, music, and me. I can't remember what the colour for my visits was. It wasn't a colour we had agreed on. But then he decided that he should have regular access to me, the same way he had access to the practice room where he played music, the gym where he went running, and the computer on which he worked, kept up with social networks, and coloured the days on his calendar. But I was on the move, I ran and lifted light weights, worked, read, and kept my own calendar.

She and I. The idea was that our time together was a gift, not a right. At least that's how I understood it, therefore I didn't insist on an explanation as to why she was staying with her boyfriend.

But the dynamic between the three of us had changed. On sports day her boyfriend was piercing me with his gaze. He played twice as hard as his teammates—he watched the ball and me at the same time. He scrutinized me with his gaze. I ran, sat on the lawn, danced. I felt free, strong, flexible. I went to the jazz concert with her, while he refused. He had backed down.

Supposedly he said that I didn't speak to him in a friendly manner. We were no longer friends. One, at most two people can fit into a small dorm room in Utrecht. *If her love is a gift, not a right, then how many ways will she be able to split it, and how much will I get?*

Every time she leaves, the weather goes crazy. Since she had gotten on the train to Dubrovnik, it's been raining nonstop. When I told my colleague from Sarajevo that she left once more, he couldn't stop laughing and said: 'Password: Dubrovnik!' He said that when people from Yugoslavia say 'Password: Dubrovnik', they mean clandestine sex. He laughed, made fun. We were sitting at an S&M bar with friends who were singing karaoke of 'What a Wonderful World'.

'You're evil, pure Satan! But you're right!' I yelled into his ear. In reality it didn't bother me that she was in the Southern sex metropolis, where many of the populous years in Czechoslovakia had been conceived. I didn't change my plans, I didn't dilute my calendar to go to summer school with her. I wasn't bothered by the idea that she was sharing a room with someone, her bed, or her kisses. She had a boyfriend anyway. But it wasn't because I was particularly open-minded. I wasn't completely selfless either. 'You like her small glasses, you're physically attracted to her, and you appreciate that she does it with you once in a while . . . It's enough for you, because there's not an ounce of passion between the two of you. You don't care, and she doesn't give a damn either,' he said.

But didn't we actually need an audience to play our passion for ourselves? My colleague from Sarajevo was the only person who knew about us. He wanted us to be a cute couple with complementary roles. He kept touching my arms to check if I had more muscles. He always noticed when I lost weight. It seemed as though he was grooming us as his erotic fantasy. But he was also our only fan, our only audience.

We could use a greater diversity of opinions, I said to myself. So I told my best friend from elementary school about us. It was a very bizarre conversation. I worked hard to tell her our story, while she only sat there and didn't say a word, didn't ask a single question. She should have asked about her name, what she looked like, what nationality she was, how we had met, and what our plans were. She didn't ask about any of it. She didn't touch the food I had set in front of her. Otherwise she had an excellent appetite—she was recently pregnant with her second child. She didn't forget to show me her maternity booklet from the gynaecologist. I wasn't particularly interested in the stamped pages. But I wanted to share her excitement. We had known one another since we sat together at school, at a desk that had my name, a plus sign, and the name of a boy from another class on it. I wished I could have introduced the two of them, and shown her how clever, stylish, and beautiful my girlfriend was. We needed an audience. I felt dependent on the people around us, on their power to approve and affirm our passion. In short, we needed people both looking and not looking at us.

My colleague from Sarajevo grinned, and he put his arm around my shoulders to prove to me that with this single gesture he could make the two of us appear to be passionate lovers. My friends reacted immediately. One friend even got a pressing need to tell me how nice and open my colleague was. I told her I thought he was cynical and malicious. But the same friend immediately started to try to convince me of his positive traits. As if she were selling him to me . . . He just laughed, downed the rest of his vodka, and left the bar. Into rainy weather.

I ran into her boyfriend in front of the library, and I almost choked on my cereal bar, which she called astronaut food. He was so shaken that he could barely type the phone number I was giving him into his cell phone. She was still in Dubrovnik. It had been raining nonstop for a week and a half. Her boyfriend and I made plans to go see a match together. 'I don't understand football much,' I said. 'But you understand beer, don't you?' he replied. He was funny and somewhat charming . . . with a little imagination and beer, he wasn't bad company. Both of us must have felt like we needed to talk or spend more time together, to work on our connection built on mutual cheating.

I wondered whether I'd ever manage to develop such a sibling relationship with my ex's girlfriend. Would she invite me for a beer? Does she drink beer? Would she lend me a book she was reading? Perhaps he had picked the opposite of me, and she couldn't read. All of the things in the apartment where we had lived together briefly and where he now lived with her had been ours and now they were theirs. The pots, the cups, the bed. The built-in refrigerator for two. The gifts we had received together. I left everything as it was. As if I had died. Everything stayed there, but there was someone else in my place.

'The thought that I could die at any moment makes me anxious,' a professor said to me, as she handed me old Slovak crowns and asked me to exchange them for her for euros or forints. She was seeing a homeopath who was helping her with the anxiety. 'It's just the sensation of freedom,' I wanted to say to her. I hadn't seen crowns for quite some time. I looked at the bulging eyes of Cyril and Methodius, the heroic profile of Pribina, and the wooden beauty of the Madonna. 'That Monopoly money of yours,' a guy from Brno said later. I converted the money using Google, and gave her forints. I rolled up the Slovak banknotes and put them with my passport and the glass heart.

I went out for a beer with her boyfriend. But our meeting was disappointing. I was boring myself, so I left. I was hungry, and I got drunk very quickly in a boring way. Later he said that he was surprised I had left and didn't come back for the final. Beer tastes the same to me during a semifinal or a final.

I bought a white carnation at a flower stand. I was on my way
to see her after she came back from Dubrovnik. It was a very
timid and harmless flower. I handed it to her as if I were asking
her to hold onto it for a moment. It matched her dress per-
fectly. A white dress from a second-hand store and a white
flower. She came on a bike. Had she been on an ad, she could
have sold me any summery beverage. After lemonade and iced
coffee we switched to beer, and then we had another one from
a can. I remembered her saying once that the taste between
the legs is like the taste of the first sip from a can.

We sipped beer, smoked mint cigarettes, and watched
teenagers on lowrider bikes showing off in the park. Both of
us liked the one in a white tank top. But she had a problem
with Hungarian men. 'Maybe this one wouldn't blather on
about Trianon,' she said. The three of us would be a different
kind of Trianon!' I said, laughing. A love triangle between a
Romanian, a Slovak, and a Hungarian. A lowbiker in a white
tank top and two nerds. We envisioned opening beer cans
together and drinking to each other's health.

'What language are they speaking?' asked some boys in
black jackets with iron-ons of the Árpád flag. She was sitting
in a pub with her boyfriend. They were talking about
Marxism in Romanian. 'Some Trianon language,' a linguist
with a shaved head said.

She told me another story. That she had dreamt about me
surprising her and showing up in Dubrovnik. She woke up
early in the morning, surprised to find herself having done it
in a room full of sleeping students. As we walked back
through a park, she lost the white flower. It must have fallen

out of her bag. We were hoping that the lowbiker in a white tank top would find it. It stormed that night, and I missed having her in my bed.

'I miss you too,' she wrote. Even though she lived only a few blocks away, she preferred to miss me. We had gotten used to missing each other. Truth be told, I wasn't sure which one of us in this story should be the one to run or bike in the rain to meet the other. Instead, I only kept meeting her that week as a green or grey symbol on Skype.

Then I ran into her boyfriend, smoking in the university courtyard. He was beaming after Russian class. He was explaining to me how incredibly difficult this language was which changed the gender of nouns, conjugated verbs, and inserted prefixes here and suffixes there. I felt like telling him: 'Yes, it's complete chaos, but you get to wake up next to that coffee-coloured body with orange-peel skin on the thighs, and I don't. So conjugate forwards and backwards, and stop complaining!'

That night I looked at my shaking cheeks in an unfortunately-placed mirror in front of a treadmill at the gym. She sent an email. We were both out of phone credit. It was the end of the month, when I usually switched to cheap canned goods, split portions in half between lunch and dinner, and ate white bread on the side. She'd stop calling. At the end of the month our romance was also running out of fuel.

And then there was a text message! It was from someone who had credit even at the end of the month! It was my colleague from Sarajevo, a doctoral law student. They never hit the bottom of their resources. They just redistributed them: porn for the people, cash for themselves. After I had eaten bread and butter for dinner, he described to me in great detail the menu he had had at a weekend conference: 'Peking duck, marinated salmon, Parma ham, and spaghetti in herb sauce. Oh, and we washed it down with Dom Pérignon!' On his way back from the conference he almost lost his passport. He dozed off on a bench in duty free, and someone took it out of his pocket. He reported the loss, and his passport was soon found. Thrown away in a flowerpot. 'Someone must have been very disappointed when he realized that he had stolen a Bosnian passport with an expired visa,' he said.

We were sitting at the same place we used to meet before. He left me nursing a glass of cheap red wine for 20 minutes, and then he showed up waving a white envelope, threw himself onto a chair, and instead of apologizing for being late, he said that he had to go to the immigration office to get a residence permit. 'Oh, you poor foreigner in the European Union!' I laughed at him. In order to make up for his unfortunate civic lot, he told me about that amazing menu. 'These conferences, these people . . . they talk about injustice and poverty and drink Dom Pérignon!' I wanted to make him feel a little guilty about the menu. 'You'll never be good enough for them with your residence permit, you know?' I added. 'I couldn't care less, as long as they're paying for duck and Dom Pérignon!' I laughed and called him Satan once more. 'Why should we suppress evil within us? Why discriminate against Satan?' he asked in a seductive lawyerlike fashion.

He was headed to the capital of vice—a university grant was sending him to Reno. 'Nevada! It's a desert! You drive for miles through nothingness, and then you run into the impossible Las Vegas. You open the car door, and it's 50 degrees. Have you ever experienced 50 degrees in a parking lot? I can tell you, it's hell!' 'If they have a pool and pay for my drinks, I don't care.' I could just picture him, sweaty from walking across the street in the hellish heat to buy some food that didn't taste like the food we knew. Put with that the sound of slot machines, rolling coins, blinking lights . . . 'Actually, I'd like to stay there, if at all possible,' he said. 'What are you going to do there? Wait until you roll three lemons?' 'And what's your plan after you finish your Long Island iced tea on Long Island?'

I hadn't thought it through that far. 'I don't have a plan. I'm hoping that I'm better than my peers, thus I'm not panicked about my work future. At least I'm trying not to be. I'll improvise.' He laughed and said: 'Have fun with that! Duck and Dom Pérignon are here and now. Within reach!'

I noticed his gold chain again, the top button unbuttoned, then buttoned again. As if he were hesitating—the Balkans or the EU. It crossed my mind that if we were to sleep together, I'd definitely ask him to take it off. 'Finally you put on some weight, that's good. Your face is still sunken, but your curves are more or less back.' The manner in which he described my swollen premenstrual body made me think that perhaps he wanted to eat me as soon as he finished his packet of Pall Malls.

Chinese duck, French champagne, and me. I liked the company he placed me in. I also liked his previous girlfriends. If we were pages in a calendar—a big lesbian from the West Coast, tattooed and with a low jazz voice; a Jewish Ukrainian extra-curly-haired activist who hugged everyone and kept flying back and forth to save the world; and a mysterious Hungarian lady, recently divorced, who supposedly yelled 'Istenem!' during climax . . . and maybe some others—which month would I be?

Spring had been quite rainy. Powerful storms, lots of wind. But it was June now, and the weather was still the same. I'll take a June like that, one that doesn't behave like June. 'Cold?' he asked as we walked from a bar, jumping over mirrors left by the rain. It was the only gentlemanly phrase I ever heard from him. But there were so many sparks flying between us that we could have caused another thunderstorm at any point. In spite of that we only kissed good-bye, cheek to cheek, and he took a taxi. I wondered how he had the money to take a taxi every time we went out. Even at the end of the month!

I sent him a text message. As I was falling asleep. He was ready to jump into another taxi. 'Do you want me?' he wrote. But by then I was asleep, dreaming, and waiting for the next morning, which would be wiser. I woke up with a clear answer to her email: 'You don't want us to be together in real life, only on the pages of a book!' I could hardly wait for her answer via Skype, Yahoo, or perhaps a text sent from her boyfriend's Romanian cell phone.

The question 'Do you want me?' had quite an impact on me. I kept repeating it to myself. If I were ever able to express my interests with such clarity, my fear of freedom would disappear.

Instead a tsunami of hormones flooded by body. I was raging, everything was making me mad. The messages I sent her had multiple meanings, my word order was scattered, I swore and used strong comparisons as a substitute for the naked simplicity of 'Do you want me?'

I chalked up my moodiness to hormones and the weather. The Danube kept rising because of heavy rains. Soon the promenade by the river was under water, as was the road by the parliament building and the tram tracks. My body kept swelling, I had the urge to eat and argue. 'I don't understand you,' I wrote. I should have plucked up my courage and written 'Do you want me?' instead. Asking this question was a lot harder than texting the guy from Sarajevo. That I keep thinking about him, a sort of 'Hold, you're in line'.

That evening she came over. She ate what I prepared, fed me a krémes cake, we drank Tokaj wine, and made love. In bed I asked her to give me a hickey, and she made several of them all over my body, but I wasn't happy with any of them. 'I'll make a map of the Kingdom of Hungary on your belly, you want?' I only wanted one hickey, in a visible place. In the morning the heavy rain stopped, my period started, and I finally gave her the glass heart.

'Do you want me?' was also the last question he asked me. After that things were clear for him. I only received gentle commands. His attention made me feel like there was nowhere to hide. Everywhere I turned, he was only one step away from me. An unbuttoned button and a gold chain with a cross on his chest.

We went to a spa together and I was drowning in his company. We couldn't agree on a single thing we'd want to do together, and yet we were always together. Satan couldn't follow me into the ladies' changing room, and he didn't have it in him to get into the ice dip. The rest was his territory: water as hot as in hell, steam, and 35 degrees outside. I could practically hear my blood rushing through my veins to cool down my body.

A jet of bubbling water pushed my left breast out of my bra. There was a hickey on it. He didn't tell me that my breast was out, he just kept talking. The breast kept bobbing on the water, as if it had decided to leave me. I kept my legs curled tight underneath me, so they wouldn't leave me one after the other. He reached out to grab my feet. For about a second I tried to decide whether I liked it or not. I took his hands in mine and gently pushed them away.

I wondered if we'd still be able to talk to each other after this gesture of mine. We did. About war movies. '*Apocalypse Now* is for people who didn't live through war. *The Deer Hunter* is much better. You don't see much happening, but it's there, you can feel it.' We talked about the mission of the Slovak foreign minister in Bosnia. 'He turned out to be a political idiot. He literally ran away from there. They even threw a shoe after him. In the long run, everyone turns out to be a political idiot in Sarajevo.' We talked about big cities. 'Paris is truly terrifying. Nothing bad ever happened to me there, but it was in the air—the state of civil war,' he said. Once again he left me to bring the beers from the bar—he threw money on the table in a wad. The top shirt button remained buttoned.

The plains near the border stretched in front of me. Miles of corn, sunflowers, and rapeseed. Without a Customs booth. I still reach into my bag to pull out my ID. And then I realize that there's no one at the border. No one cares about it any more. Go, whoever, wherever.

I started to think about my ex in sentences that sounded like folk song lyrics:

Don't ask me to come to your wedding
Don't set a plate on the long table
Don't fell a tree, spare a cow
Because I won't come
I'll never come back again
You put your bride in my bed
Let her make you a bed of roses.

I needed to hear something that would make me see *Apocalypse Now* as a two-dimensional story with too many special effects. I needed his secret. I said to her: 'I'll sleep with Satan to shake out his secret from him. I need to know what he did during the four years that Sarajevo was under siege.' She suggested that I go see the exhibit of exhumed bodies from Srebrenica instead. I needed to shock myself to such a degree that I could finally sleep. A full eight hours with my eyes closed. I needed his story so much!

———

What follows love? Its opposite. It's not a joke. The opposite of love isn't hate. So many people told me: 'You should kick your ex and his new girlfriend out of your apartment!' In the 'Little big town' I became 'the girl who lets her ex live with his new girlfriend in an apartment she had decorated for him and her'. Contractors. IKEA. Gifts from family. A fridge for two. I woke up in a small room in my parents' apartment feeling so angry that at breakfast I broke my tooth on a fork. I searched my mouth and wrote her about this next tooth event. The tooth fragment disappeared, it was gone. Suddenly my smile looked different in the mirror.

'My God, I'm always looking for something!' grandma said with a sigh. She saw me walking with my bags from the train station. She immediately set the pots on the stove. 'Me too,' I said. Then I cried on the balcony, but she brought me inside to cry at the kitchen table, because that's where women have cried since time immemorial. She did the talking: 'Some designer hanged himself in a closet full of dresses he had designed. Naked. My colleague's husband hanged himself. She came home with bags full of spelling tests and found him on the chandelier. That's how it goes! But have a good cry.' When she finished, I thanked her. She said that she told me all those things just to make me feel better.

'Thank you, as men say after oral sex,' she wrote to me in a chat and added a smiley face. She could joke about bodies and their functions, walk naked around the apartment or the beach, stay home for days reading thick novels, or eat two *krémes* cakes for breakfast. She could always make me feel better. And once again she was gone. I went back to the 'Little big town' to vote for the 'Roma initiative'.

To liquefy our next parting, we drank two pitchers of margaritas. She didn't remember pedalling home on her bike, and I didn't remember turning on loud music and not turning it off until the wee hours. We both remembered kissing passionately outside my building. We barely paid any attention to the passers-by, and miraculously, they paid no attention to us. But then her body pedalled home, that is, to her boyfriend, and mine blasted some heart-wrenching melodies. The bed was cold, but I woke up sweaty. I searched my mouth with my tongue, to see if the tooth fragment hadn't turned up.

We touch everything only with our tongue. She wrote to me about poststructuralism, which she had recently dusted off: 'They say everything is language. We're trapped in language. There's no outside.' I wished to get rid of my native language, and throw him, 'my baby', out of my head like water from a bathtub. I'll have to reinvent myself. For example, as a Jewish woman who speaks English with an unidentifiable Eastern European accent. Or I could be a White Gypsy. I have so many lines on my palm that I could be anyone I want. She leaned over those lines to tell me my path, loves, and children. 'But it's the left hand that gets read for fortune telling,' I said to her at the end of our chat session.

The bus window was showing the countryside: calm fields, yellow and green. A three-hour documentary. Between Slovakia and Hungary lies the flattest of land. A pancake. 'Of course, you're working out your own personal Trianon (read: a rotten compromise),' the Sarajevo guy wrote in a text. So I did it. I met with my ex and asked him and the lady to move out. Even so my chest felt heavier. 'I feel as if I were carrying sacks of potatoes. It's really, really hard,' I said. Sitting next to me, he didn't say anything. And then he did say something: 'I don't know what to say to that.'

Pouring love from one place to another is like filling a bathtub by carrying water in your mouth. From then on I was able to formulate what I had only suspected: *That was love, and whatever would come after it would only be—an after-love.* The root of the word disrupted by a prefix. Its pure form stayed in the kitchen section of IKEA. Kötbullar, striped bedding, and a built-in refrigerator. 'Go water the home happiness', that's what grandma called the plant in the corner of the room. I kept waking up before sunrise, and had to change my T-shirt, the front and back of which were soaked in sweat.

'Think about the worst thing that has ever happened to you, and come tell me about it; tell me something terrifying,' I wrote to the guy from Sarajevo. I was ready to listen to real war stories. Not stories from field manoeuvres, but from war, where they shoot real bullets at people doing crosswords. But he, who had lived through Sarajevo, wrote that he was depressed and couldn't talk. He said he took a pill and was about to lie down.

Instead of a war story he told me that the extreme heat over the weekend, which he had to spend at his desk, had put him in a bad mood. I wanted to cry. He had nothing to tell me. 'How about we go to Aqualand?' he asked instead. Then he suggested that I join him and a couple of other people on a weeklong trip to Lake Balaton. Dom Pérignon was coming too.

———

She wrote from Bern, and immediately left for Krakow. She was a little disappointed that she didn't get accepted into the summer school in Trent, but thankfully she got confirmation from Andalusia. She planned our time for a week in August. She kept moving, meeting people, eating sweets across Europe. 'But I miss krémes,' she wrote. Her boyfriend had stayed in Budapest, watched the World Cup, and wrote about the relationship between football and capitalism. His Russian vocabulary was quickly expanding, but I still had a better accent.

As we stood at the edge of the dance floor at a club, smoked, and watched the dancing couples, I wasn't sure which one of us was feeling more sorry for the other. He told me what the followers of the Frankfurt school thought about football, and I shared their views on disco with him. It occurred to me that we should talk about her. At the same time I didn't have the energy to deal with another Trianon. 'Do you want to dance?' I asked. 'I don't dance. Do you want a beer?' he replied.

'Trianon is a good metaphor, I like using it,' the Sarajevo veteran said. 'Someone should write about it, don't you think?' Then he started to expound on the topics the book could cover and how the chapters should be organized. 'And you could contribute the article "Trianon in Personal Relationships",' he said, laughing. 'Do you have a light?' I extended my hand towards him. He tossed me a lighter. If we didn't smoke, we'd have nothing in common. Her emails sounded like voices from afar. I could hear an anthem through the wall. The game was over. Someone won. The university hallways emptied, the marble had an echo. Ambulances and fire trucks swirled the hot air.

'How are you?' 'Miserable.' 'I love misery. I love your misery,' she Skyped. 'It's the latest trend of 2010!' I turned over my credit card, copied the three-digit security code, and paid for a ticket to Bucharest.

DELTA

'So, at the International Conference on Elephants, the British present a three-volume encyclopedia, *All About Elephants*. Next, the French present a single volume, but with a provocative title, *The Secret Life of Elephants*. Finally, the Hungarian delegates take the stage with a pamphlet entitled "Elephants and Trianon".' This was the joke she told me as she barrelled past the train station.

'Oops, I didn't stop. I'll stop on my way back.'

The national nightmare: an image of failure, injustice, loss of coordination, misalignment of geography, and dissolution of self-confidence. That's the definition my colleague from Sarajevo came up with. My personal Trianon was coming back early the next day. I still had bad dreams, but they were less frequent now. He was the one who wrote: 'It hurts, but you must go on.' I wasn't sure where exactly his *on* led. Where was this place I should have been going? Hadn't I been going enough? Wasn't that the real problem?

I got on a plane. She picked me up at the airport and put me in a cab. From Bucharest she drove to the last port on the Danube. After that, we had to take a boat. A river express on the way there and a steamship on the way back. In Sfântu Gheorghe, a minibus went back and forth to the beach at unpredictable intervals. It was really just a covered trailer pulled by a tractor or a jeep. The rest was on foot. All the way to the end of the continent. In the sand, every step required extra effort.

'This is the newest country in Europe,' she said.

We sat down on a strip of beach, one side of which sloped into the sea and the other into the Danube. Branches, seaweed, shells, even the damp sand—everything was fresh. We were sitting on freshly-baked Europe. It's ironic that Europe was expanding in Romania. There was a campground close to the beach, and across from it was a military base, guarding the new Europe. You couldn't go any further. Beyond was just water, nothing else.

Once more she asked me how I was, how I felt. 'Speak, use some modifiers! Express your feelings! How do you like it here?' The Delta was the most impressive place I had ever seen. Three branches of the Danube empty into the sea there, and the sea is barely salty. Seagulls fly over the river, and fresh-water birds fly over the sea. Instead of asphalt, the roads are made of powdery sand, and they lead to the beach. We were in paradise. I wanted to be madly in love there. Maybe she wanted the same thing. But we just lay next to each other and talked. We swam and we ate fish. We were having a good time. Not a bit better. But that was plenty.

———

I gave myself the summer as a present for my birthday, which I had completely forgotten about during the winter. I was in the 'Little big town', at my parents'; I came back and they said,

'You're home'. I ended up between a tower of boxes filled with my things and the things my parents had moved there during my absence. My grandmother put me on a 'one-warm-meal-a-day' plan. Exercise lost its former urgency. Old girlfriends kept popping up, I made plans with each of them, but had no time for any of it. I was home. More so than ever before, because this time, I was just passing through. Neighbours addressed me in the informal whenever I took out the trash. Some of them still remembered my name. Some were no longer there. I was afraid to ask. I always wanted to find things the way I had left them. The stars in the night sky seemed to have found peace and stopped. The clouds nuzzled up to the featherbeds hung over the railing. I stood on the balcony, romanticizing.

'I'm afraid to leave the house. It's not my home any more. I don't want to run into anyone,' she wrote. She didn't see eye to eye with the people she had grown up, gone to school, or been friends with. Some of them accused her of taking the easy way out by leaving. Others grumbled about everything, and said she had done the right thing. Yet neither of us had left. We hadn't packed up our suitcases in the middle of the night, we hadn't swum across the Danube, nor had we climbed over barbed wire. We were simply doing what everyone else was talking about: 'Nowadays you can travel, go to good schools, meet people, and speak with them in a foreign language . . .' We wanted to be a part of it, to engage with the world. To eat it with a big spoon. To break our teeth on it. We weren't abandoning anyone or anything. If we had, then only sym-bolically. The Romanian Marxist had supposedly abandoned the bourgeois ways. Now he indulged in social critique and Marlboro reds. She had abandoned the obligatory heterosexual notion of romance, and took off in search of her ideal woman. She'd get oh-so-close to finding her in this or that summer program, but she had yet to meet the wealthy Italian with a villa, who could afford her a life of leisure with academia as a hobby. She'd be like a Gypsy in hog heaven.

'What about you? What do you want? Where will you be in a couple of years?' she asked me. We were lying in the powdery sand, pushing clouds across the blue sky with our eyes. She had the books for her summer program in Andalusia under her head. I had Erica Jong's *Fear of Flying* under mine. Feminist summer reading. I had picked it out from her floor-to-ceiling library. 'I don't want anything. I've got it so good, that if I put it in my status, I'd immediately lose all of my friends.' Maybe I wanted to be the Italian with a villa and a lover. For the time being, I was just a shy substance, out of which she was forming her ideal woman. 'Take everything off! Swimming naked feels incredible!'

I took off my swim top, and I was a bit disappointed to find that it didn't cause a world revolution. She laughed and calmly walked naked to the end of Europe, where she submerged herself in the border waters and swam towards the horizon. I took a sip of my beer, but it only gave me enough courage to flop from my belly onto my back.

'So you're in love?' she asked. Passion showed up in the most unexpected place. I was telling her about a guy I had met at the wedding of my best friend from elementary school. The friend had lost all patience with me. 'Do you even like him?' she asked, exasperated. She had a little boy in her arms, and a little girl in her belly. I kissed the best man, and then I chased him until he asked me a completely inappropriate question: 'Want to make a baby?' I stroked his hair. He finally chuckled. When I told him how I had voted, he took me to the Museum of Roma Culture. We laughed at the saying 'Murš murš, džuvľi džuvľi'. A man is a man, a woman is a woman. In the morning I had to get up to catch a train. It was time to move on. To go after her. To the end of the world, all the way to where Europe curves, turning its back on the East.

'I like him. But we wouldn't get along,' I said to one as well as the other. 'He thought breakfast was a code word for menstruation.'

It was her fault. After I left for the wedding, she wrote: 'I want you to enjoy yourself. Eat, dance, and flirt!' So I ate hot peppers, danced the waltz, and kissed the best man. She should have commended me. When we saw each other in Bucharest and I was talking about him, laughing after each sentence, and blushing, she asked: 'So you're in love?' I fell asleep before she got back from the bathroom and lay down next to me. I slept on the beach, after meals, in the car, even on a couch at the Museum of Natural History.

I was finally able to sleep, especially at dawn. I have no idea what sunrise looks like in the Delta. When I woke up, the sun was high, and the room was filled with heavy, salty air. In a daze I asked: 'Should we get up or keep sleeping?' She didn't answer. Instead she reached for the alarm. I closed my eyes and drifted over the horizon, naked under the covers. I had just enough wherewithal to realize I had uttered the last sentence in Slovak.

It was payback for her sleepwalking tendency. She was the one who had asked me 'What time is it?' in Romanian when we woke up in her light-filled apartment that first night, in her bed barely big enough for two. As if her boyfriend had been the one next to her. Suddenly it didn't matter who was there, whose soft, friendly body it was. We're so replaceable it hurts! 'I spied on your ex. I think his new girlfriend looks like you,' my best friend from elementary school told me. She said what I wanted to hear from a friend.

'We're close, which is why we want to speak in our native languages,' she explained. At night and in the wee hours of the morning we'd keep coming home from a foreign language. *I'm home, what time is it?* In the Delta my watch stopped and my cell phone broke. At the end of the continent, one time zone east of Central Europe, it was as if all measurements were falling off the end of the world, which was flat. She leaned over me to study my forehead. We were past words in our native languages. All we had were gestures. She gestured *I want you.* I leaned over her back: *I want you.*

Locals stood around on a neighbouring towel island and kept staring at us. One island past them was a naked guy whose gaze was fixed on the sky—a gaggle of geese was giving him thumbs up. At the fast food stands, stray dogs kept staring at our plates. 'You have to push through. It's like making love in a room with a crucifix,' she said. I laughed; we walked down an unpaved street in the dark, bugs crunching and frogs squishing under our feet. We leaned against each other in bed, and decided to stop worrying about the landlady in the next room. 'This is my very good friend,' she introduced me to her. The icons gazed into the darkness with their large, hazelnut eyes. She has eyes like that. We were getting up early the next morning to catch the steamship.

I finally got to see a sunrise in the Delta. Words turn off like cell phones here, and the mind stops like a watch. Finally she stopped asking me how I felt and how I liked it. She pressed her head into my shoulder and dozed off. The ship set sail, the passengers were still. Half-asleep, they whispered to each other in a jumble of native languages: *What time is it?*

———

I like him because he understands passion. He sends me the results of card tournaments. He keeps losing, yet he's really enjoying the game. 'I wouldn't take care of the baby anyway. Whenever I have a little money, I spend it on cards,' he said. I wished him good luck in the game. He understood me, waved, and the train moved. Direction Brno–Kúty–Bratislava and Brno–Kúty–Vienna.

'This is supposed be first class? It's an ice box!' someone said and kept walking through the train car. The train split in two in Kúty, and took the malcontent in his warm train car directly to Vienna without stopping in Bratislava.

Vienna in the spring of that year. In March, revolution was in the air at the university. She got excited about the student cause, and I got excited about a trip to see her. Walking from the train station I joined a crowd of protesters, the front of which shouted slogans in German and Italian, and the back conversed with the policemen. Perhaps the protesters were asking for directions to the university, where to get good beer, or where to find a cheap hostel.

At long last I found the revolutionary headquarters. She showed me where the bar was, and where she had set down her things. The Italian anarchists hadn't slept for three nights. Someone was playing the piano in the middle of the room. Political videos ran in a loop. People engaged in discussions and exchanged contact information. She showed me the occupied auditorium. 'Just peek in there, it stinks of something fierce.' Since October the students had been occupying the auditorium with seats as uncomfortable as those at Cinema Nostalgia. They quietly moved out when the auditorium was rented for commercial purposes and the university threatened to take them to court. Then they reoccupied it.

In the morning, the headquarters was cleared out; students in work brigades were washing the floors. Then they scattered into their discussion groups according to a posted schedule. I sat in one that was reading a manifesto. An interpreter who had been assigned to me, the only non-German speaker, kept whispering into my ear. I watched an eloquent, handsome, Turkish-looking guy in Gucci glasses. 'You'll be the first to go work in the boiler room when a world revolution breaks out,' I thought. 'They'll take away your stove and you'll have to cook on an electric burner at the neighbour's,' I foretold about a female student in similar glasses. Murš, murš, džuvľi, džuvľi. Maybe not this time. Maybe it'll work out this time. We'll all ride a train where they don't just heat in first class. There'll be a little bit of heat everywhere. Just enough. Somehow.

'Could you turn on the heat?' she asked a classmate we were staying with in Vienna. 'What's his deal? Look at him—he's educated, works at the university, doesn't have insurance, and scrimps on heating . . . It won't be much better in 10 years.' He turned up the heat, but we were still cold. Pressed up against one another, we laughed and exhaled beer. 'I feel sparks around here. Should we do something about it?' After such a romantic invitation, I could hardly resist the call of the sexual revolution. 'Well put,' I said. I wanted us to keep our standards even in revolutionary conditions. I was a little worried about our classmate in the next room. She misunderstood me: 'If he wants to, he can join us,' she said. 'He has a curved bird. I've never seen anything like it. I couldn't believe such a thing existed. Seriously!'

In the morning, she took a bus back to Budapest, after making both of us—me as well as the classmate with a curved bird—breakfast. 'Don't bother, I like to do my own thing in the morning,' said he, the bourgeois individualist. I'm sure he was just pretending that his tasty Nespresso machine was broken! 'I got it for my 30th birthday. I'll go exchange it tomorrow.' He let me buy him a coffee at a kiosk and we split a croissant. Then we each went our separate ways to our discussion groups. Inspired by the strong sentences of the manifesto, I wrote short but striking verses about her soft, coffee-coloured body. She tasted fair trade. Nothing on her was curved, missing, or extra. Beauty was evenly distributed over her whole body.

The question of the fridge. I placed it between the women's question and the Roma question. 'You don't know how to look,' my mother used to say. 'The fridge is full, and you can't find anything to eat.' One time, my ex filled the built-in fridge for two; it was full of delicacies. He even put sunflower seeds in the pantry, two packets no less. And then he said it wasn't for me. That night we broke up. My whole political agenda shrunk to a few empty slots on the calendar and the sound of a car engine.

Sunflower seeds are good for fighting depression. I read that somewhere, and then I told him about it. He bought two packets; he was well stocked to be able to send me away, because I was away all the time anyway. Between Hungary and Slovakia there were fields and fields of sunflowers.

The best man's fridge was empty; there was only a bowl of spread in it. 'Have some!' he said. He had jams in his pantry. 'Have some. My mom makes them and no one eats them.' I ate a strawberry jam in one sitting. 'Name what you want, and I'll make it for you,' he wrote. 'A hot dog in a bun,' I blurted out, and he rented a hot dog maker. I was eating a homemade hot dog with extra mustard and drinking beer. The taste of the hot dog immediately set off my chemical equation of happiness.

I wondered why I shouldn't stay sitting there forever. Hold a hot dog and just be happy. Then lie down next to a warm body and warm it up some more. 'You're burning up,' my ex used to say. 'Do you have a fever?' she asked. 'You're quite warm!' the best man said. He packed a jar of strawberry jam for me. 'Don't. I'm traveling. I can't take it with me.' Customs would throw it in the trash. Customs agents pretend they don't know what jam is and treat it like an explosive. Then again, he didn't know what jam was either. 'Oh, preserves!' That sounds a lot closer to explosives. I just didn't want to travel with jam.

Her mother had filled the fridge with delicacies like roasted peppers in balsamic vinegar, grape leaves in tomato sauce, a cheese platter, aubergine spread, and tomatoes as big as a worker's fist. All of it was for us. She set it out on the table in front of me. Plus a dish of caviar. Right next to the fridge was an espresso maker. I could have stayed there pressing the cappuccino button forever.

We went to get the car washed together. Before our trip to the Delta we bought groceries, watered the houseplants, and went to a car wash. We waited on the curb and watched people walking along one of the big boulevards of Bucharest. When we got in the car, she ran her finger over the dashboard. She was not happy. Furthermore, the cup holder had sunflower peels in it, which hadn't been there before; the person who washed the dashboard must have been eating sunflower seeds. I wrote her name in the dust on the dashboard.

I like watching her drive, make up her own road rules, talk, change radio stations, and gesticulate. I used to like watching him too: hands on the steering wheel in the ten-and-two position, he'd shift gears, switch a CD, make a call. 'Don't answer it,' I'd always say, and he'd always answer it. On our car trips together, I felt a deep sense of peace. I was in motion, and at the same time I was sitting next to a beloved person.

It was pleasant letting myself be shown around. We drove on the large boulevards of Bucharest, and she kept showing me: 'That's where everyone goes to eat in the morning after going to the clubs,' 'Over there is a victory arch modelled on the one in Paris,' and 'I went to school there.' The card player took me around Brno; sometimes he'd take a sharp turn to show me where they have the best Pilsner on tap, where he went to eat in the wee hours, and where he had gone to school.

Outside the car window, the countryside looked flat and empty. I had gotten used to seeing hours upon hours of flat land on the roads between Budapest and Bratislava. Colourful, naked, muddy, snow-covered. But this wasn't just flat land, it was a wasteland. When we opened the door at the last port on the Danube, we were hit by terrible heat and air that smelt of water. 'Every time I come to the coast and walk in this heat, I ask myself why I came. And every year I get in the car and come back,' she said.

The only way to go further was on water. The ship was like an overheated bus floating on its belly. The metal gleamed, the leatherette seats kept sticking to us, people sighed. The ones who were seated were falling asleep from the heat in poses that looked like scenes from a massacre.

In the harbour we bought a beach umbrella and a ball. Wind turned over our beach umbrella, and we forgot the ball in one of the two bars in Sfântu Gheorghe. With the same verve she had battled the wind for the umbrella, anchoring it in the sand and turning it as the sun moved, she went in search of the ball. 'What are you getting upset about? A ball is for children. We gave it to some kid. Come back tomorrow, maybe it'll turn up.' That's what they told her at the food stand where we had forgotten the ball under a bench.

We went back the next day. If I wanted passion, I could have watched her slam her fist on the counter, yell, and keep repeating *mindže*—ball. As she was leaving, she cursed the food stand owner's whole family down to the last generation, and she didn't calm down until nighttime: 'Serves them right, the village bums, that capitalism came, at least they'll stop stealing and start working!'

I used to be politically braver. I had an opinion from Guantanamo to backpackers in India, from slave ships to the female workers in maquiladoras, from the Twin Towers to the trash island in the Pacific. Everything was connected; a gentle harmony of injustices and privileges was woven into an almost mythical view of the world. I was angry, curious, engaged. I loved getting into debates, ready to talk politics with anyone while waiting at a bus stop.

That was when I first noticed how my ex was looking at me. Maybe he felt embarrassed. As if I had lifted my skirt and peed in public. Not even squatting, but standing up. 'What are you trying to do?' he asked me once, sounding almost exhausted. I had scorned the things he enjoyed; I didn't close my eyes in bliss over homemade sushi, nor did I draw detailed plans for where to place the couch.

I kept squirming, taking everything apart, walking up and down, sometimes to the postbox to pick up a leftist rag. 'You can finally read *Slovo* without interruptions,' he said, outlining my post-breakup agenda. And yet he had also been searching. He read *No Logo*, went to India, snuffed a box of cocaine in a week, and got into running with such enthusiasm that he read everything Google had to offer on the subject. He kept searching in me too; during our best lovemaking he spoke my name. As if he were calling me, for me to come to him from a distance, to come closer and stay. *You're home!*

'What do Slovaks say when they make love?' Satan's question made me laugh every time. As if we should be singing the national anthem or reciting patriotic poetry. I leaned over to him and whispered: 'Istenem!'

At an exhibit on Dracula and vampirism in Bucharest, we stood in front of a painting of Erszébet Báthory. 'We have to go to that exhibit, even if it's tourist kitsch. Everyone will ask me about Dracula at home, because no one knows anything else about Romania.' 'Look!' She showed me her slightly pointy canines, not unlike those of every other mortal.

She took notes and laughed about the ancient works that had studied the habits of vampires, witches, and other underworld creatures with utmost interest. 'It's just like the current study of terrorists,' she said, laughing and showing those unexceptionally pointy teeth. 'What if our dissertations are found like this someday? They'll be put on display and people will walk around, laughing about the things we studied.'

In spite of this thought, we were able to get up in the morning and go to the library. We sat in silence for hours. Both of us were able to get up from a hot bed with rumpled sheets, wave to each other at the airport, and go where our latest stipend sent us. We'd walk down into artificially-lit rooms where every step had a triple echo. In the semi-darkness we'd surround ourselves with volumes of books. Then, in a state of anxiety and half-madness, we'd start writing our dissertations: *Life and Habits of Vampires in Lower Ugria*. We let everything around us flow like a river. Outside people kept getting old and multiplying . . . That must have been how he saw me. *What are you trying to do?*

For the time being, we were just sitting on board a steamship. Her head on my Picasso-like square shoulder. She was awake, not because of insomnia, but because of the morning freshness of a new day before a trip. We had walked down a dusty path to the harbour to catch the steamship from Sfântu Gheorghe to Tulcea. We sat down on the upper deck, and then we just watched the water carry us away and the sun rise. The Delta was lined by trees that didn't have green, but silver leaves. In the deep silence, only the ship's engine could be heard. Someone told us that we'd see pelicans early in the morning. Maybe they'd fly out, maybe not.

A Frenchman who had gone to the Delta to ring birds talked to us. He told us what he studied, what he did, where he was headed. 'We catch them in nets, then we ring them, and then we release them.' He asked us where we had met. 'Look, look, pelicans! Over there!' I exclaimed. 'Just kidding. I'm going to get coffee.' When I came back, she was still talking to the Frenchman.

⸺

'What do we say to each other?' she asked at the airport. As she drove to the airport, I was still shaking from our recent lovemaking, as if I had just arrived on a train on the Istanbul–Stockholm route. We didn't even have time to kiss. We spent our last minutes listening to a guy who said: 'How good to hear someone speaking English!' The words flew out of him, he practically had verbal diarrhoea: he had to pay for overweight luggage, he was on his way back to Canada, he understood Romanian, had dual citizenship, his parents fled right after the Ceauşescus were shot, he was sweaty and needed a shower. We stood in front of his story, not knowing what to say. He wanted to know who we were. We looked at each other, waiting to see which one of us would use the very-good-friend line. There was silence. He put out his cigarette and dragged his suitcase to the terminal.

What do we say to each other? The glass doors opened, and a group of Orthodox Jews streamed into the terminal.

'Go, they're waiting for you,' she said with a smile. 'You're really not Jewish? I think you should be,' she whispered into my ear at check-in and nomaded away. Her next stop was Andalusia. The hot sands of Spain. 'I'll dust off my Spanish!' I didn't know she spoke Spanish.

For a while I roamed around the duty-free shops. I hadn't had time to shower, so I put on two or three brand-name perfumes. The airplane lifted my innards, held them in suspense, and then released them. I spent a moment on the usual airplane thoughts, such as how such a pile of metal can fly through the air, why the sky is blue, and whose name would I shout if we were falling. *What do Slovaks say when a plane is falling?* Then I just read until we landed.